Nature Boy

Mike Herring

Mike Herring

Mike Herring

FIRST EDITION

GREEN CAT BOOKS

www.green-cat.co/books

Mike Herring

CONTENTS

Mike Herring

ACKNOWLEDGMENTS

DEDICATION AND THANKS TO MY WIFE VALERIE
FOR HER LOVE, SUPPORT AND UNDERSTANDING
DURING MY MANY LONG VENTURES AWAY FROM
HOME ON LOCATION FILMING THE LIFESTYLE

ONE

In the year 1933, Gilles was born in the rough brick farm house tucked into the wilds of the mountains that divide France and Spain. On his third birthday his father had introduced him to his first bow and arrows and had proudly watched him struggle to draw the bow back. Once having mastered the bow, the two of them set off into the wilds hunting for game as that was the only way they could survive. They were off to stalk wild boar that day. Gilles had been told to follow behind his father and keeping windward so as to avoid letting the boar have scent of them. The sun was high in the sky and hot on their naked bodies, for they had no need for clothing. Gillies had never come into contact with civilisation as the mountains are wild and they were miles from any form of human life. His mother and father had lived like this ever since they were young – nude and free with nature and only wearing clothes when the weather demanded. Hunting and fishing was their life. They grew their own vegetables and wheat corn to make bread. There was a spring that provided them with pure fresh water for drinking, and the waters that cascaded down from the highest point of the mountains are dammed so as to provide a bathing area for summer and winter. Gillies cut a fine young figure even at the age of three. His body was a darkened brown and his hair long like his father. He had strength in his body and his muscles were already forming. His feet were toughened, although his father had made him a crude pair of sandals made from animal skins with thongs that cross tied around the calves of his legs. Today they had been fishing when they heard the wild boar amongst the thick undergrowth amongst the trees. His father had raised his finger to his lips to hush Gillies from making a noise. With his gun held half cocked, his father made his way around the rock pool and beckoned Gillies to follow. He watched his father crawl on all fours across the rocks so as to approach the boar with the breeze in their faces. He imitated his father movements and stayed close behind him for he knew that the boar could attack them if he were to pick up their scent. His father had shown him scars on his arms where he had been attacked by one a few years ago. He was a strong healthy man with a body that was weathered against all weathers toughened by his nakedness at all times. As they entered the undergrowth his father beckoned him to remain still. They both listened, for now they were close to where the boar was shuffling around for food. Gillies popped his head up above the bush that they were crouched behind, where he could see the boar. He gasped, and his father placed his hand over his mouth quickly. The gun was raised and his father took aim. The sound of the gun echoed around the mountainside like thunder. Gillies watched as he saw the boar attempt to make a run towards them, but it stumbled and fell within seconds. Once again, his father had taken only one shot to kill his prey. Gillies went to run forward, but his father caught hold of his arm. He knew that often a boar would make a final bid to attack, but this time he lay motionless. Gillies gave a whoop of joy as he drew his bow and fired an arrow into the neck of the boar. He was already a good marksman. His father ruffled Gillies hair, then handed him his gun to carry. His father stooped down and tied some crudely made thongs around the legs of the boar bringing them together, then with one mighty shout of joy, he heaved the massive size boar up over his shoulders and headed for home. Gillies walked proudly behind his father carrying the gun as if it were his. Mother greeted their return. They had been out since early morning with having only bread and goats cheese to eat. She stood there in the doorway watching and waving to her two men of nature. Gillies ran forward into her arms. His mother took the gun he had been carrying and gave him a cuddle in her arms and nestled his head against her naked bosom. He felt safe and secure in her arms.

"Look what father shot," he said, with a grin that stretched from ear to ear. "I shot it too with an arrow."

His mother kissed him on his cheek, and then turned to greet her husband and helped him relieve himself of his heavy load. They had meat for a month at least, and fish galore. His father hung the boar up by its rear legs, then with one swift slash of his knife, the boar's throat was cut and the blood drained away into a vessel. Gillies stood in the doorway of the outer barn and watched this without even a turn of his head, as he had seen this done many times before. Back inside the farmhouse they sat down to a bowl of hot potato soup and freshly made bread. Outside the sun was still quite hot, and so once Gillies had finished his meal, he begged to go outside and swim in the man-made pool. He loved swimming underwater as it was so clear, but better still he liked going down right to the foot of the mountain where the water formed a waterfall and where he could walk under the overhanging rock-face, letting the water cascade over him. As he was so young, he was only allowed to do this when his parents were with him. The night time was also exciting for him as he like to sit outside the farmhouse watching the stars above him. Quite often he and his father would lie there watching the shooting stars. Even at his tender age he did not feel the chill of the night approaching. He was content to remain naked until his mother called him to get ready for bed. His bed was built up in the pitch of the roof. He loved this room as he could look down from his single bed and over the handrail, knowing that his parents were down below. Once the oil lamps were turned off and his parents were in bed, he could still see around his little room as the moonlight filtered through the fanlight window above his bed. He often lay there listening to the sounds of the mountain streams and the call of the wolves on the prowl. These were the sounds of the night, sounds that he had learned not to fear. One day he would be a big strong man like his father, and would be allowed to hunt and fish on his own. He often dreamed that he had a gun of his own, and could shoot as well as his father. Then he could let his father rest more, and he would be the hunter bringing home the food. He wanted to be big and strong like his father. He often watched him chopping wood for the fire with an axe. Those powerful shoulders washed with sweat that glistened in the sunlight. Would he be as strong as this? Now that he was five, coming on six years of age, he started judging his own body as against the body of his father. The hair on the chest would surely come one day, he thought, as he ran his hands across his own bare chest. He often wrestled with his father in fun times, and felt the power that his father had stored up inside his body, but he was always curious about the hair that grew in certain ways on his father. How long would it be before hair started to grow? There were many things he had to learn about life yet. His mother had started to teach him to read from the few books that were shelved high up on a shelf by the side of the fireplace. He loved to listen to her soft voice reading to him at night. They would sit together on the sheepskin rug in front of the log fire, their warm naked bodies bonding, giving him that feeling of being wanted and loved. His father would watch as he sat there, smoking his pipe, in a crudely made wooden chair. They were a contented family.

The mountains were remote, and Gillies had never met people. His life was sheltered from the world out there across the mountain range. His friend became a deer he had found suffering a broken leg. He had pleaded with his father not to shoot him and provide them with more food. His father, seeing his son's tears and concern for the deer, carried it back into the shelter of the cabin. Gillies watched the skill of his father as he bound the fractured leg in splints. Gillies named it 'Bambi', having heard the name from his mother's reading from books when he was three. Bambi was bedded down on straw in an outbuilding. Gillies had to be dragged away from his new friend when bedtime was the call of the day. He couldn't sleep at first in his bed, so when he knew that his parents had retired downstairs, in their own bed at the end of the main room, he crept down the crude ladder that served as stairs, and bedded down with Bambi. For the first three nights, he managed to stay awake and returned back to his own bed. However, as the week went on, his tiredness overcame him, and he was found by his father, in the early hours of the morning, with his head resting across the neck of Bambi. His father smiled at the scene, and left Gillies to sleep. Within four weeks Bambi was ready to have his splints removed. Gillies helped his friend to stand naturally on his own. There were shouts of joy as Bambi stood, a little unsure, but unaided. Gillies and his father walked out of the outbuilding and towards the cabin… Bambi followed. That first day was a long day for Gillies, as he feared that his father would try to encourage Bambi to return to the forests up in the mountains. His mother refused to allow Bambi into the cabin, but it was difficult trying to keep him out.

The day was dawning. Gillies was already with Bambi out in the yard watching him running around. Their fun was suddenly ended, as he saw his father approaching with what he suddenly realised was a rope. Gillies watched his father place a rope around the neck of his friend.

"Come son. We will have to return him to his natural home."

"Don't do that father, I want him to stay."

 "Come son. It is best."

They had talked many times about this day. Gillies had tried to not believe it would happen. His father bent down and picked his son up in his arms, but Gillies turned his head away, as he didn't want his tears to be seen. The climb up the mountainside and into the forest was not easy going. They reached the area where they had first found Bambi. Gillies knew this was the moment he had been dreading. The rope was taken off, and they all stood frozen to the spot. Father clapped his hands together to usher Bambi away, but he stood there, bewildered and motionless. Gillies looked up at his father appealing to him to take his friend back home. His father walked a few steps away, turned and offered his hand for Gillies to hold. Gillies knew that there was little use in trying to change his father's mind. As they made their way back down the mountain side, Gillies kept looking back over his shoulder. Bambi was still standing motionless in the same spot. The two of them sat down on a fallen tree trunk for a while. Gillies shielded his eyes against the sun, and in the distance he saw Bambi take a few steps away from them, and started to feed himself on the fresh green grass.

"There you are," father said, "see, he is happy to be back in his own home now son."

The day was not a happy day for Gillies. He had been fishing with his father, and although they had swam together, he didn't respond to playing around in the lake.

They sat on the rocks as usual, letting the sun dry their bodies as they cast their lines to catch fish. Gillies thoughts were with his friend up in the mountains. That evening, as they sat outside eating their fish supper, Gillies was constantly scanning the area around the cabin for sight of Bambi. He went to bed early, not waiting to have to be told to do so. His little world seemed to be empty now. He slept in short drifts of alertness for the faintest sound of movement outside the cabin. The sunlight of a new day drifted through his skylight window, warming his naked body as he lay there on top of his blanket. He silently got out of bed and crept towards the wooden rail that ran the length of the small loft. He peered down below to where his parents slept.

He rubbed his eyes. Below he could see the broad back of his father and his buttocks in motion as he knelt astride his mother. At first, he looked away from the scene below, but his curious mind urged him to look again. What he was watching was a strange act that his young mind raced to make sense of, for there was his father with his penis now stiffer than normal, entering it in and out of his mother's pubic hair area. He lay there watching, for this was new to him, yet in a way it all began to make sense of the feelings he had been getting of late. It also reminded him of the time he had seen Bambi's cock as it grew in size for the first time. His young mind, at the time was, unable to deal with this sight. Now as he watched his father's cock actions, this seemed to react on him in several ways. He was nervous just in case he was caught watching the scene below, but he could not stop watching, as it was both frightening, yet exciting to watch. Then Bambi flashed through his mind, and the time he had watched that small string like cock grow so large, it had frightened him on seeing this. These two scenes now began to make sense of the strange feelings he had experienced many times of late. There had been those nights where he felt his cock grow, and he was tempted to touch it, in a different way, that brought a strange tingle of excitement through his body. He had studied his father's body many times as they had shared the days hunting and naked together. They were close and at ease in each other's company. His father, although not overly hairy, had hair under his arms and a bush of hair around his *cock,* as they called it. When he looked down at himself, at his tender age, there were no signs of hair on his body. He had asked his father if he would have hair too. He remembered being told that he would one day, and then he could call himself a real man. This reply was followed by a swift shove of his father's hand, and his ungainly dive into the water of the lake. His head was clearing now, and the many unanswered questions were becoming clear. He lay there, looking down at his parents now, curious as to how it would all end. They seemed to writhe and kiss. His father seemed to give a lurch at one stage as his actions quickened. There was a sound of joy as the two strained away. His father called out something, as his mother placed her hand over his mouth to smother his voice. Gillies ducked his head back, not to be caught watching. His father had looked over his shoulder and up towards his son's bedroom. Then there was silence. Gillies dared a look down again, just in time to see his father withdraw and lie back on the bed and pull the blanket back over the two of them. Gillies crept back to his own bed, and thoughts rushed through his head. These thoughts were short lived, as suddenly he heard sounds outside the cabin. He clambered out of bed again, and without thinking hurried down the wooden ladder. He glanced across the room towards his parent's bed. His father waved a hand, as if he had been woken by Gillies. He waved back as if to be surprised that his father was awake so early. He opened the door excitedly, and there stood his friend, tail wagging and body trembling with joyous movements of being united again. He took Bambi back into the outbuilding, and filled the bucket with water. He sat down in the straw watching his friend lapping the water down. Bambi then joined him, and the two friends curled up together. Gillies wondered what animal's thoughts were, or if they really did think like humans. He had his own thoughts running through his head. Being six was not easy. He had seen many times the animals in the woods and mountains playing together. The images of these playful scenes crossed his mind.

He had seen the stags mount others. How could their cocks grow so large, and why? He looked at Bambi, he had seen his friends cock get bigger at times, but he had no other deer to mount like the other wild animals in the mountains. He touched himself; yes, he had had moments like that. His thoughts then went deeper. Those stags had cocks, yet others didn't. He suddenly sat up straight. His mother was different from his father. So what they were doing in bed that morning was exactly the same as the animals of the wild did, but why? His thoughts were disturbed, as the shadow of his father's body drifted across the small outhouse floor strewn with straw.

"What are you doing out here?"

Gillies fell across the body of Bambi, almost in fear that his father would once again take his friend back into the mountains. He looked up at his father with that look of fear in his eyes. To his surprise, his father knelt down and patted Bambi on the neck, then ruffled Gillies mop of dark hair. Gillies knew there was hope for Bambi, with the affection his father was showing them both. Gillies moved, and threw his arms around his father's broad shoulders. No words were needed, Gillies felt safe and secure.

"Can he stay?"

"He can, that is until he hears the call of nature out there."

Gillies, at the time, only heard those words *'the call of nature'* but they meant nothing, they were just words.

TWO

As the months passed, Gillies and Bambi roamed the rugged mountainsides. They wandered further from the cabin on each venture of the wild. On one of these carefree days, Gillies had climbed to one of the highest peaks. The view was amazing, as he could see for miles and miles. As Bambi roamed around eating the sweet green grass, Gillies sat there eating the bread, and cooked meat, that his mother had insisted he took with him. The sun was high, and he shielded his eyes as he studied the horizon. There was a bright flash of light way off in the distance, and then nothing. He blinked, as he had never seen this before. He stood up and looked back into the direction again.

Yes, there it was. The light had moved a little to his right though. Gillies strained his eyes for sight of the light again, but it was too far away for him to see what it was that was reflecting the sunlight. Later that day, on his way back to the cabin, he rambled through the undergrowth to check one of the two rabbit snares that he had set up. This means of catching wildlife he had learned from his father, but this was the first time he had set these traps by himself.

He approached the first of them, making sure that his feet never stepped on fallen trigs from the trees or acorns and cones. This was a well-rehearsed routine that he was carrying out now. He knew the trap was some way ahead of him, and so he every step was made with caution. What he had not taken into account was his four-legged friend. Bambi had not rehearsed the same routine. Suddenly there was a loud crack, the sound of snapped branches as Bambi followed Gillies through the undergrowth. Gillies slapped his side loudly, and looked angrily back over his shoulder. Bambi froze on the spot, almost as if he knew that he was at fault. On inspecting the rabbit snare, Gillies sighed, the snare was untouched. He took the simple snare apart, and moved away from the undergrowth. He took hold of Bambi's neck and led him away towards the second snare. This time he tethered Bambi to a tree some distance away. Stealthily, Gillies once again approached his second snare. Step by step, with arms outstretched like wings to balance him, he approached the spot. To his delight, there, before his excited eyes, a rabbit lay with his neck through the noose. As he went to stoop down to take hold of his catch, the rabbit moved slightly. Gillies stood frozen to the spot. He was not prepared for this.

He could not just leave the rabbit to die a slow death. He had seen his father place the final blow to an animal to put it out of pain and distress, but he had never attempted this on his own. He looked around for a sturdy bow of a tree. Holding it in one hand, and taking a deep breath, he brought the piece of wood down with such a force on the side of the rabbit's head. His other hand at the same time forced the animal's body down on the ground. He felt the blow shudder through the body. He felt sick. He had closed his eyes at the point of impact, but now he had to look at the result. Yes, the rabbit's life had been ended with that one fatal blow. He took hold of the rabbit's hind legs, and slung its body over his shoulder. As he returned to untie Bambi, he could feel the warm blood from his catch, trickle down his naked back, but he was not bothered as he was now a proud hunter. As he approached the cabin, walking tall and proud, he saw his father first as he swung an axe at the logs in the yard outside the cabin. Gillies raised his catch high above his head with pride, waiting for some form of reaction from his father. His father looked up for a moment; he smiled, and then continued with his task of wood chopping.

"Look at my catch," Gillies called out, as he raised the rabbit high in the air.

"That looks a fine one," his father said. "Now you have to skin it, lad."

Mother came to the cabin door. She was pleased to see her son returned home safe and sound. She walked towards him and put her arm around his shoulders. She gave him a hug and planted a kiss on his forehead.

"What have we here?" she asked, looking at the proud face of Gillies.

"He found it in the woods asleep." Father called out.

"You get on with your wood chopping. You are slowing up in your own age," his wife replied. "At least we have a son who brings food to the table."

Gillies felt quite proud now on hearing that. Now he had to skin the rabbit. His father had shown him how to do it, but this would be his first time. He laid his catch out on the wooden bench, and with his knife he made his first cut. He was aware that his father was watching between his axe swings. With the first cuts made, Gillies then started to remove the rabbit's fur, revealing the pink skin. He felt he had done well.

Now he had to remove the innards. By the time he had finished, he looked a bloody mess. His mother pumped water into the wooden water bucket, and he washed his body clean with the cold water. As he stood there drying himself with the rough sackcloth towel, his father joined him to rid is own naked body of toiled sweat.

Gillies told his father about the light reflections he had seen across the mountain range far away. His father took time to reply.

"Well lad, there, far away, there must be other people living out there. Best not wander so far from now on. We don't want any of them coming over here do we?"

Gillies shook his head, but in his mind he wondered why. He had never given thought to the fact that they must be other people out there, but now, having been that close to finding out, his young curious mind would not rest there. As he sat there that evening watching the rabbit roasting on the fire outside the cabin, his thoughts were still with that glistening light across the mountain range. He watched as his mother rotated the roasting spit. He studied her body. She seemed to be plumper around her waist, but it was her stomach that was getting more rounded. The rabbit made for a good meal, and even his father praised him for his fine catch. As Gillies ate the meat and potatoes from his white enamel plate, once again his mind started to ask questions. He looked around the cabin and started to take notice of the various objects. The enamel mugs, father's treasured shotgun hanging on the chimney breast. These had all come from somewhere, as his father could not have made all these things himself. He looked across the table at his father. Dare he ask him, or would he be told not to ask?

"Father, where did all these things come from?"

"What things?"

Gillies held up his drinking mug and gestured by waving it in his hand. He watched as his parents exchanged glances with each other.

"Well son, we brought these with us when we first came here to build the cabin."

"Where did you get them from?"

"The town, many hours travel from here," his father said, pointing out through the window.

"Is that where you go sometimes with the cart?" Gillies asked, with the image of seeing his father last year sitting high up on the cart, and slapping the reins across the buttocks of *Dobbin,* their trusted shire horse of many duties. He had watched his father and the cart disappear down the rough track. He had been gone for two days, so the town must have been a long way away. He also remembered seeing his father wearing clothes for the first time. It had made him laugh, watching him struggle with putting his trousers on, and the hopping around the cabin trying to get one leg into them. But where was this place? Would he ever see the town for himself? He wasn't lonely or sad being alone in the wilds of the mountains, but was now curious as to what lay beyond the furthest point he had wandered so far to catch the rabbit.

After the meal had finished, he took one of the books from the shelf, and flicked through the pages, looking at the pictures as he lay in bed. Although his mother had sat with him for many an hour reading to him, he still struggled with understanding the words himself. He pondered over some of the pictures that showed men and women holding each other in their arms. On one page, two young people could be seen kissing. Yes, his mother often kissed him, but these two were of the same age, probably about twice his age, he thought. He looked around to see if his parents were watching. He kissed the back of his hand. Huh, he felt nothing special in that, he thought. But, there had been times that when his mother kissed him, he had felt warm, secure and comforted. He kissed the back of his hand again, but felt nothing. His mind was now beginning to make enquiring signals in his head. He had been born in the cabin, and knew nothing more than what nature was teaching him. The stags in the forest clearings, with cocks firm and long, playing games, like mounting each other's backs. The ones being mounted were without cocks. So that is what he had seen often with his parent's bed. It was the same as the deer in the forests. Then there was Bambi. He too had a cock that grew long and hard, then went down again after a while. It was all beginning to make sense in a way, for he too had begun to experience his own cock getting hard. At first, he had been scared that something terrible was happening to him. But seeing how it was with Bambi, made him feel better. Maybe this was alright to be this way. Now though, he was feeling more than good about having a hard cock. He had many a time touched himself there, worried as to what was happening to his body. Now though lately, these touches had sent a weird yet exciting sensations running through his body. The book fell to the floor, and sleep crept in, as he could no longer keep his eyes open. There were so many questioned unanswered still running around in his head, and his sleep was mixed with dreams and feelings he had never experienced before. He felt a hand on his shoulder, and he awoke with a start. He looked up to see his father kneeling at the side of his bed.

"What's the matter, son, you have been crying out in your sleep? You are hot."

Gillies turned away from his father for a moment, not wanting to let him know that he was experiencing strange feelings in his body. His father patted him on his head, for he knew the troubled mind of his son.

Mike Herring

THREE

Although the month was November, the winter days were still warm. Gillies was shown how to use the axe to chop logs for the winter fires in the evenings. He could feel the strength building in his arms as daily he took over more and more of this work from his father. He admired the strength in his father's body, he was a powerful man. He too was seeing changes in his own body now. As he rested for a while, he studied his mother as she went about washing the bedclothes in a tub of water. Her waist had expanded, and her stomach was now beginning to bulge. She looked tired at times. She stopped many times to wipe her brow. His father more often carried the bucket of water from the well for her. This was never the case in the past, as she had often refused his help, but now she was pleased of his offers. His father had noticed Gillies studies of his mother. He knew that he had to explain what was happening to her to expand like this. He had to do this soon, as the baby was due in about a month's time.

He also knew that he had to reassure his son what was happening to his body. Many a time he felt guilty of living the way they did, alone, as a family unit, in the remote mountains, so wild, yet so peaceful. Now that Gillies was approaching his teens, maybe he should introduce him to the large world out there. Both he and his wife had done their best to help their son to read and write, but there was more to life than that. Gillies had to learn about life. He no longer could protect his son from the outside world. But how could he start to explain all these things? The need to stock up with food for the winter months was approaching. They had plenty of potatoes and cabbage from their garden, but the meat was getting low in the out shed store. It was time for the two of them to go hunting. They set off armed with bow and arrows for Gillies, whist he carried his heavy shot gun. Gillies had been promised that on this hunting trip he would be allowed to use the gun. Mother watched the two men in her life head off up into the forest, high up in the mountainside. Once up high into the forest, they started to build a shelter for the night. Gillies was always amazed at his father's great knowledge of nature. He had worked out where the sun would rise, and built the shelter so that the entrance would receive the most of the sun's warmth. Boughs were cut, and pine leave branches were laid across the structures to form the roof. The firewood was collected, and his father showed him how to spark a light for the fire by rolling a stick between his palms into the hollow of a log. As soon as the friction showed signs of smoke, Gillies blew the first sparks gently into the dry straw, and with gentle puffs of breath, suddenly a small flame appeared. Soon the fire was in full blaze. Enough wood had been collected to keep a steady fire alive whilst they explored the surrounding forest for wildlife tracks. Snares were set to catch rabbits, and on their way back to their shelter they saw signs of deer droppings. His father had said that they would rise early in the morning to hunt the deer. They were approaching a clearing, when his father caught hold of his arm, and beckoned him to remain still. They crouched down low into the heather. His father pointed ahead of them. There they could see a herd of deer moving slowly through the lush green grass. They heard the roar of the stag, as this powerful beast searched the herd for mating. Gillies had seen the act in the past, but he was about to learn his first facts of life. His father watched Gillies face as the stag made his selection of females to mount. There was never a moment of unease between the two of them, this was nature, and this was natural. They both watched the stag mount, and his penis enter. The action was swift, yet full of power. Soon the stag retreated and roared his success, the sound of this roared around the forest and beyond.

"Wasn't that great?" his father said.

Gillies smiled and nodded, but no words passed his lips. His thoughts flashed back to the night he had seen his parents perform the same act in bed.

"Do you know what the stag was doing?"

"I think so," Gillies replied. "I saw you and mother doing that one night."

There was a silence between them for a while. Gillies felt the strong hand of his father push him over into the undergrowth. They laughed and wrestled together.

"You little bugger!" his father laughed. "You have been watching us make a baby so that you will have a brother or sister to look after."

Gillies giggled. This was all becoming clear now as to what was going on in his own body. He wanted his father to explain a little more, but the herd of deer had suddenly stampeded away from the clearing. His father stood up suddenly, his gun cocked and firing.

One of the deer fell. There was sudden panic amongst the herd as they swung around to change direction. They were gone, apart from the one his father had skilfully shot, so fast, so accurate. They ran across the clearing, his father taking his hunting knife out of its sheath as they approached the fallen deer. Gillies watched as the swift slash of the blade across the neck of the deer, and it lay there not moving now. This was nature in the raw. The deer was food for the table. He helped his father tie the deer's legs together with rope. A strong length of bough was the carrying rod that threaded through the rear and front legs of the deer. Gillies was not tall enough yet to make the removal of their kill easy. His father teased him as he struggled with the weight. Back at their shelter, the deer was strung up high into a tree nearby. That evening, as they sat around the fire, the subject of the stag mounting was raised. Gillies sat there as the facts of life were explained to him. Now Gillies understood why his mother's belly was getting bigger. He also now knew what the strange feelings he was now getting in his own body were all about. He laughed as his father stood with his back to him, peeing into the bushes a short distance away from the shelter. Gillies joined him. They stood side by side. He was feeling a man now. His father looked down at his own flow of pee.

"You see, down there is a seed also, not just pee. When you want to make babies like the stag, and your mother and me, you let that seed out, and it grows inside your mother. There are lots of seeds that come out all at once, and one seed will find a friend inside your mother, and they will hold onto each other, and make a baby for us."

Gillies watched his father finish his pee and shake his penis. It was quite big, which matched the strength of the rest of his body. He was a strong man. Gillies looked down at himself as he tried to shake his own penis like his father. His father ruffled his mop of dark hair, and smiled at his son. He was proud of him, and he was also pleased in the way he had been able to explain the facts of life in this way. There was a lot to be learned through being with nature this way. They placed logs on the fire to help keep warm that night in the shelter. Gillies mind raced over the words of his father about making babies. He pictured in his mind the way the stags mounted the females, but not before their penises had grown long and firm. His own penis began to stir as he thought about the scenes he had witnessed. He touched himself, and it felt good. His hand stroked his rising hardness, but he became scared that his father would see him. He sat up to see if his father had moved from around the fire. He called out to see if he was coming to sleep in the shelter, but there was no reply. He lay there tempted to continue stroking himself. Soon he began to feel strange feelings that almost took his breath away. To his horror, there was a sudden strange feeling, and it scared him. The strange feeling reached a peak, his breathing was erratic, and he felt a little dizzy. He released his hand away from his stiff penis in panic. Sitting up suddenly, he was relieved that his father had not seen him, he was still sleeping. Surely there was something more than this that had to happen before babies could be made. Maybe you had to pee at the same time. That's it, he thought. Sleep did not come easy that night; he had not drifted off easily, or assured that he had answered his puzzled mind. Morning light appeared, and the sun cast its warm rays on his naked body as he lay there in the shelter. He turned his head to see if his father was still asleep. There was no sign of him, and the fire had burned itself to ashes. He shuffled out of the shelter and gathered a handful of twigs. Placing them on the still hot ashes, the fire sparked into life. Soon the fire was ablaze again, the heat felt good on his chilled body. He stood up and looked around for sight of his father. He stood and took a pee on the spot he and his father had shared the night before. He heard the cracking of fallen branches from the trees; he looked in the direction to see his father appearing from the forest. He waved, and his father waved back as he held high two rabbits that had been caught in the snares. They ate stale bread from the sackcloth food bag, and drank the herb tea that had been brewed in the metal pan over the fire. Once breakfast had been taken, they smothered the fire with earth and prepared to leave for home. They were at least half a day's walk away from the cabin, and the weight of the deer they carried caused them to stop many times to rest. His father teased him about his height, yet he was proud of the way Gillies was growing into a young handsome man. He also teased him about the first signs of pubic hair. Gillies punched his father on his muscular arm for teasing him, but he was beginning to feel a young man now with body hair appearing.

As they eventually caught sight of their cabin through the edge of the forest, they could also see mother waving in the distance. The family was reunited with kisses and embraces. Gillies was teased by his mother about his long, tousled hair wanting to be trimmed. His father laughed aloud as she also tugged at his long hair as well. He in turn teased her about her now rounded tummy. He placed his arms around her and his hands felt her roundness. They both laughed as he felt the movement of their new baby as he or she kicked away inside. Gillies was told that he could also feel the movements. At first he was almost shy to do so, but was happy that he was able to feel and understand what was happening inside his mother. He felt the sudden kicking movements. He laughed and suddenly found himself telling his father that he was a clever man. The two of them smiled at each other in knowing fashion, they were going to be great friends and share many facts of life together.

FOUR

Gillies sleep was broken by the sound of his mother's cries in the night. He sat up in his bed, then rubbing his eyes with the back of his hands; he hurried to look over the rail of the loft that was his bedroom. The oil lamps were burning below, and he could see his mother laying there on top of her bed, writhing in pain. He hurried downstairs.

"Hurry!" he heard his father call out. "I need lots of boiling water, and get me some towels, quickly boy."

Gillies stood there for a moment unable to move. His mother was in pain, and he knew the baby was due to be born. Part of him wanted to stand and watch, but he knew that he had to obey his fathers shouted orders. The big metal kettle was placed on the fire. Towels were found from the drawers of the cabinet. He returned to his mother's side. His father looked worried as he tried to encourage his wife to push as the head of the baby appeared. Gillies stood there watching, a little scared, yet excited. He knelt down to hold his mother's hand. Just for a moment she smiled for him.

"Hot water, boy.'" his father demanded.

Gillies dashed back to the boiling kettle and returned with a bowl. He watched as his father reached out to hold the baby as it arrived into the world. He felt useless at this point, and found himself staring at his mother, and wondering how on earth she was able to be stretched so much to let the baby out like that. He had seen young deer being born out in the forest, and had watched as the new life lay there as its mother cleaned her new born. Now he watched his father cradle the new born in a towel and wash her. Yes, it was a girl, he had a sister. His father smiled as he held the small bundle in his arms proudly. He looked at Gillies who was watching bemused by it all.

"You have a sister." He said, watching as Gillies went to his mother to kiss her for being so brave. The baby was handed to his mother, and almost instantly, his sister sucked on the nipples of his mother. Gillies had seen young deer sucking the teats of its mother. He had milked the goats, and now it was all becoming clear to him. Once his mother had fed his sister, she handed the new born to

Gillies to hold for the first time. His heart beat faster as he felt the body contact, so warm, so natural. His parents watched with pride. He laughed nervously as his little sister kicked and wriggled in his arms. His father had made the bottom draw of the chest into a cot, padded out with warm blankets and cotton sheets. She slept. That night, Gillies sat with his parents on their bed, they talked about the day. Names were discussed, and they eventually agreed on Charlotte. The fire crackled away as logs were added to keep the cabin warm and cosy. Gillies kissed both parents and his new sister Charlotte goodnight; it had been a long night. He retired back to his bed up in the loft. He lay there under the blankets just reflecting back on the events of the day, his knowledge of life near complete, yet there were one or two things that still played on his mind. How was it that he had no seed coming from his own penis, yet he had all those strange feelings inside him, and was becoming more erect every day now?

The following days and weeks saw changes in his daily life. Bambi had to be released into the wilds again and this was going to be difficult to do. Charlotte demanded more and more attention from his parents, which meant that he had more chores to do than usual.

The wood chopping, and water carrying from the well was helping develop his body, and muscles seemed to develop quickly now, and he was beginning to feel a young man. He became aware that hairs had started to appear on parts of his body. The first time he had noticed this was when swimming in the lake one afternoon. As he lay there letting the sun dry his body, he felt hairs on his legs as he rubbed them. The search then began. Yes, there were signs of pubic hair, and hairs under his arms.

On his return back to the cabin, his father was waiting for him. He looked stern.

"Gillies, Bambi has to be returned to his forest. Sorry son, but he has been wandering into the cabin and has taken food. Now that Charlotte is moving around, he has been trying to play with her, and your mother is frightened that he might harm her when left alone. So today you have to release him."

Gillies looked sad, but he understood. He asked if he could take him back to the wilds in the morning, as he wanted to take him to the far side of the mountain range, and that would be a day's walking distance. That night he slept on the hay in the outhouse with Bambi. Next morning, with a rope around the neck of Bambi, he set off with enough food and water to last the trip. He looked back at the cabin. His mother and father stood with arms around each other, watching him. They waved, and he waved back. They all shared the sadness of the situation. The sun was now rising and warmed Gillies back, but soon he would be deep into the forest, and the warmth of the sun would be lost. They walked for four hours, stopping only to drink water when Gillies found small clearings where the sun broke through. He had talked to Bambi most of the time, trying to explain that what he was about to do in releasing him into the wild again was for the best. In his own heart and mind though, he was going to feel alone and sad. It was midday, and the sun was high. This was the moment that he had to release his friend back to nature. He removed the rope and stroked Bambi on his neck. To his surprise, Bambi dashed away with his hind legs kicking high behind him. Gillies watched his friend disappear through the trees. He stopped for a moment, standing proud with head high and alert, looked back at Gillies, and then he was gone. This was not what Gillies had expected. He felt suddenly sad about their parting. He walked to the edge of the clearing in the hope that Bambi would race back to him. His eyes searched in every direction, but there was no sign of his friend. As he stood there, quite numb with emotion, suddenly he saw a light flashing across the valley as he had once seen before in that direction. He remembered his father's words, telling him not to wander into that direction, but he felt this light drawing him towards it. It was only sunlight reflecting, but there must be life over there. The sun had moved way to the west now. He had to hurry as time was running out for him. He ran naked and free through long lush green grasses and trying to avoid the patches of bracken. He ran like an athlete, his body so fit, and now so manly, for he was now a young man in his flush of youth. The flashes of light were no longer visible as he was now down in the valley. As he started his climb up into the direction of the light, he suddenly began to feel insecure, for he had never met other humans, other than his parents. The books he had read were the only reference as to what was out there in the world beyond. He looked at his own nakedness. Never had he seen in the books naked people, for they were all wearing clothes. He had once or twice tried wearing his father's clothes that he worn only to go into the outside world for supplies. They had been far too big for him, but he had felt the roughness of weave against his flesh, and he had felt uncomfortable and trapped within them. Not for him, he was happy with his nakedness, the way he had been born. But now, he was unsure what he would find as he approached the area of the light. In front of him now was a copse of trees. He approached with caution. Through the clearing he caught sight of log cabins. He could hear the voices of people. Ducking down low in the undergrowth, he approached, not knowing what he might find. His father's voice echoed in his head, but he had to find out for himself. Was this the place that his father drove the cart to on his trips out? Suddenly he caught sight of other humans. He lay flat down now, his eyes searching the scene. There he could see groups of people, some sitting on stools, and some standing. They looked just like the people in the books back home. There were women and girls dressed in long skirts and wearing bonnets on their heads. His mother had spoken of such women. There were men and youths standing around laughing and talking. The men smoked pipes and drank from jars with handles. As he looked beyond the first group of people, he could see a long rough road full of wheel tracks. People were walking and entering the stores and returning with goods to load on the carts, with horses tethered to the railing. All he could see now he had seen in his books. So this was a town. He suddenly felt scared. He had to retreat and get away quickly as he didn't belong to this world, and his father had told him so. He scrambled his retreat through the rough undergrowth which tore at his naked flesh. Soon he was able to stand up and he started to run back down the valley. His tracks were brought to an abrupt halt as he was about to leave the shelter of the woodland. To his horror, right in front of him was a young girl of about fifteen or so. He froze on the spot. The girl covered her mouth with her hand as she stared at him, and he at her. For a moment they stood still just in silence. Gillies mouth was dry, but he tried to speak.

"I'm sorry." he spluttered, yet made no attempt to cover himself, as he was natural and knew no difference.

"Who are you?" the girl asked, "and where do you come from?"

Gillies was unable to speak now, and pointed across the valley and up to the forest beyond. He started to walk past her, but she seemed not unnerved by his appearance. "Don't go just yet." she suddenly said, looking around her as she spoke. 'I have never seen a boy like you before."

Gillies didn't quite know how to react. He stood there with his confidence returning.

"Do you live in the wilds up there?" she asked, not taking her eyes off him.

Gillies watched the direction of her eyes, they were not just concentrated on his nakedness, they searched his face, and he began to feel uncomfortable again.

"I live with my family up and over the far side of the mountains."

"Why do you not wear clothes?" She asked.

"Why do you wear clothes?" He replied.

They were both shocked by their own questions and she showed signs of a smile.

"Where do you go to school?" She asked.

"School, what's school?"

The girl looked shocked.

Gillies had read or heard the word before, but never even thought about the meaning.

"Where you go to read and learn." The girl explained, putting her hand to her mouth again to restrain a laugh.

"Oh, I do that at home, my mother reads to me."

"Where is your village?"

"I don't live in a village; I live just with my family."

"Why no clothes?" She asked again.

"We don't need them."

"You mean your parents don't wear clothes either?"

Gillies shook his head. He studied the girl she was pretty, yet not shy. Suddenly there was a call from the distance. The girl looked suddenly nervous.

"That's my mother calling me. I have been away too long. What's your name?"

"Gillies, what's yours?"

"Charlotte."

Gillies laughed aloud. The girl looked alarmed at his mirth.

"That's my little sister's name. I think it's a nice name."

Charlotte smiled. Then she heard her mother call her again. She began to walk away but Gillies could see she wanted to stay.

"Will you be here tomorrow?" She asked.

Gillies replied that he would. The answer had been without thought, as to if it was possible to be there the following day or not. There was something strange going on in his head, and he didn't know the reason for this. He wanted her to stay longer, but she moved away, as she did she reached out and touched his shoulder as if to prove he was real. He stood there unable to move and watched her start running through the trees. She turned, waved, and then was gone. This had been the first person he had met or spoken to in his life and his whole body was responding to it.

At first, he just walked at a slow pace, looking over his shoulder just to see if Charlotte was there again. He then started running, he ran so fast that he found his lungs gasping for air, yet he felt that he needed something to release the pent-up feelings he had within himself. He had never felt like this before. His mind went back to the books he had read and the stories about two young people meeting and falling in love. Was this what it was like? Was that all there was to it? They hadn't kissed like he had read about. The only contact was when she touched his bare shoulder. Once he could run no more, he was able to collect himself and think again. He would find the shelter he and his father had made and sleep there for the night, he would then return to find Charlotte in the morning. His parents would worry about him though, but he was now a young man…well nearly. The shelter still stood there, a little weather worn, but would provide shelter enough for the night. Now all the skills his father had tried to teach him came into play. First to get a fire lit for the night to keep him warm. He was lucky as he found the piece of wood that was used before. He found a twig, some dried grass and small pieces of wood and set about the task of twisting the twig between his hands. He worked the twig for ages and just was about to give up when a small ember started to give heat. With much care, he placed the dried grass to the ember and blew gently until the grass became alight. Soon the fire was burning well enough to place some larger logs on, and the glow warmed him in the chill of the evening. He was hungry. He unwrapped the cloth that held the food his mother had prepared for him.

There wasn't much, as he hadn't expected to stay away all night, so he halved the food so as to have some left for the next day. He sat alone with his thoughts. He couldn't get Charlotte out of his mind. The evening crept in, and the sky lit up with stars. He laid there trying to count them, but Charlotte kept crossing his mind. He rested his head on his hands, but he had a great temptation to hold himself as his penis grew hard. He smiled as once again he was going to excite himself by working his hands on it without anything more than a sensation lifted him high, only to be let down with no more than a feeling of guilt for doing this to himself. He lay there, going through the motions as he had many times before, but this time there was something else that was happening to him. He found himself wanting to rise to his knees and arch his back as he worked harder on his erection. The sensation that followed caused him to call out aloud into the stillness of the night. With legs wide apart, he watched as a white fluid shot from his shaft. It was the most wonderful sensation he had ever experienced. His head spun around as he let the spurts flow. At last he knew the meaning of life. He stroked away until it became impossible to keep going… He didn't want the feeling to leave him. Was it going to happen this night anyway, or was it that he had seen his first girl. The face of Charlotte appeared in his head again. Yes, it was her that had made it possible. He sat there thinking about her and what had happened. His whole body shook with the experience. So that was what his father enjoyed on the many nights he had seen, watching him making love. He smiled to himself, he was learning fast now about life. For a moment he had a mix of emotions, guilt, nervous curiosity and joy. He yawned and lay down under his shelter and suddenly felt tired. The night was cold, and sleep did not come easy. Morning arrived and greeted him in his shelter with sunshine. The events of yesterday flooded his mind, and a sense of excitement made him wake to the morning. He stretched his limbs as he stood up in the early morning sunlight. A touch of guilt crept back into his sleepy head. He felt scared for a moment as he felt the remains of the dried up fluid on his body from last evening. He ripped some dew soaked strands of grass and wiped his body clean. He didn't want Charlotte to see any signs of what he had done. Was it too early to head off to see her?

He suddenly remembered seeing a stream somewhere near the clearing through the trees. He hurried his way through the woods trying to remember where he had seen the water that trickled down the mountainside. He was hungry, so he picked at the wild blackberry bushes for handfuls of their fruit to satisfy his hunger in part. Once he had found the little stream that trickled down over the rocks, he took handfuls of the cold water and washed his body clean. He now felt alive and ready to face the world. Back at his shelter he drank the last of the water and ate the last of the now stale bread. The sun had risen high in the blue sky as he set off to find Charlotte. He was excited, yet nervous at the thought of seeing her again. As he approached the wooded area where he had met her, he hid low in the tall grass out of sight. His eyes searched constantly for sight of her. The sun had now moved around high over the trees, which told him that it was midday. As he lay there his thoughts were about seeing someone wearing clothes. He had never ever been conscious of his nakedness before and had not thought about Charlotte seeing him this way. It seemed ages hiding in the long grass, and then suddenly he heard the sound of movement through the trees. He parted the grasses, his eyes searching for sight of her. There she stood, her head turning and looking around her. He sat up and their eyes met. She smiled and waved, and at the same time put a finger to his lips to silence him if he were to call out. She approached him, and sat down at his side.

"Hello," she said, "I hoped that you would be here." She smiled at him.

"I wasn't sure if you would come." He replied.

There was a silence between them as their eyes admired each other.

"Does your mother know where you are?"

"No." Charlotte laughed. "I think she would be horrified to see me with a boy with no clothes on."

"Do you mind seeing me like this?"

Charlotte shook her head as she smiled.

"You are the first boy I have seen like this, I like it." She said, almost blushing.

Gillies smiled, as he knew no other way of living.

"I think it's nice being like you are. I wish I could be like you too." They sat there just looking at each other, both happy at what they viewed. Gillies felt completely at ease as he started to explain his life with his parents in the mountains. Charlotte listened in total silence. Her mind raced away with her.

"I would love to swim like you in the streams." She suddenly found herself saying.

Gillies sat there completely dazed by this sudden outburst of words. He reached forward to take hold of her hand, hoping that she would not reject him. Charlotte held her hand out to receive his. They laughed together, both feeling nervous, for they hardly knew each other. Her hand felt so soft in his more nature hardened hand. She looked at him as she examined his hand.

"You are strong I can see." She said. "Will you take me to your stream?"

"Yes of course, but what about your parents, won't they be worried?"

"They won't know if we swim in the moonlight.' She smiled.

Gillies felt happy, oh so happy. But in his mind he had to think how long he had been away from his own parents, they would be worried. He leaned forward to kiss her. There was a youthful clumsy attempt to kiss. Yes, their lips touched briefly, just long enough for Gillies to feel that magical feeling of youth's first kiss. He felt good.

"Yes, let's swim tonight. I will wait here for night to fall."

Charlotte looked flushed on her cheeks. She looked away for a moment in the direction of her village. She stood up and brushed her dress down to remove the grass.

"I will be here as soon as the sun goes down. My parents are going to the village hall for a meeting of the elders this evening. I will let them see me go to my bedroom and then I will come to meet you. Have you food and water?"

"No, but I will be alright."

"I must go now." She said, looking in the direction of her home.

They attempted to kiss again; they were clumsy once more but laughed at themselves.

Gillies watched Charlotte make her way back to her home. He lay down again in the long grass, his body shaking a little with excitement. He had been aware that his penis had stirred a little, yet now it resumed its normal shape. He smiled and lay flat on his back looking up into the sky. So this is what happens, he thought. It was a good feeling. The sun was beginning to sink lower in the sky now, and he once again began to feel excited that soon Charlotte would return to him. Whether it was through hunger or the long days wait for night time to arrive, he was found by Charlotte asleep curled up in the long grass. He awoke by the touch of her gentle hand on his shoulder shaking him. He opened his eyes; his vision was not clear as it was now dark.

"Come on sleepy head. Look, I have brought you some food and something to drink."

Gillies sat up suddenly rather taken aback by being woken so suddenly like this.

"Oh sorry, I must have dropped off to sleep. Did I hear you say food?"

Charlotte laughed as she handed him the little bundle of bread and chicken, all wrapped up in a cloth. He thanked her and immediately took a bite out of the bread, he then tore off some of the chicken leg, and oh God was he hungry. Charlotte watched, amused at the way he ate without stopping for breath.

"Here, take some of this wine."

"Wine, I have never had wine, only water."

Charlotte looked hurt. Gillies on seeing this took the vessel and took a mouthful of red wine. It hit the back of his throat like a ball of fire. He coughed and they both laughed at his antics. He drank some more wine and then he continued to eat the bread. Charlotte knelt there, watching his every move. Having refreshed himself a little, Gillies stood up and reached for her hand. His head was a little fuzzy at first. They made their way up into the mountain and towards the lake. They had very little to say at this stage of their friendship. They were quite some way off from the lake when

Charlotte suddenly stopped, released her hand of Gillies hand and started to remove her dress. Gillies watched, not embarrassed, but more in relief that she was joining him naked in the night. He had only seen his mother naked, but there was something that stirred him on seeing Charlotte's young body with breasts not quite yet completely formed. He could not help looking at the smooth roundness of her young stomach and buttocks. She also had begun to show signs of pubic hair, but hers were fair as against his own jet black bush.

"There we are, nearly there. Look over there, can you see and hear the waterfall?"

"Oh, I feel so free at last," she called out aloud. She kissed him on his cheek.

Gillies dived into the cool water first. He broke the surface and saw her standing on the rocks, not too sure that she could dive in the same way as Gillies.

"Jump, come on jump in, it's great in here."

He watched as Charlotte took a deep breath and held her nose, then jump into the lake, calling out aloud at her newly found freedom. Soon they were splashing around and swimming, diving under the surface and reappearing from nowhere. Each knew what they wanted out of this evening together, yet both were innocent about life. Nature has a way of showing the way in life's troubled path and this was going to be their first introduction to it. As they surfaced they reached out their arms and embraced. Their kiss was no longer clumsy. Their bodies entwined as one, as they struggled to stay afloat. Gillies loved the feel of her now firm breasts against his chest. He had had no one to tell him what was right or wrong in what they were doing or what to expect. Charlotte arched her body backwards and cried out into the darkness of the night. Gillies found himself wanting to kiss her breasts and caress them with his hands. The first touch and first kiss sent a shudder through his body. His own natural erection had not been noticed by him at this stage, although he was feeling a sensation so new and exciting. He sucked at her nipples, it seemed so natural and such a nice a thing to enjoy. It was when he felt her hand touch and hold his erect shaft, that his interest in caressing her body subsided for a moment. This wonderful and beautiful feeling of someone other than himself touching and stroking him was so wonderful and exciting. It was for what only seemed seconds before he was aroused so much that his love juices erupted in gushes to both their joyous youthful innocence. They had no idea as to what was happening to them both, but it seemed so natural, they just lived for the moment. The moon and stars above lit up their nakedness as they rested on the rocks, having reached this erotic high of innocent youth. Gillies had been tempted to enter her, as he had watched his father and mother that night, but he was scared as to what would happen. He had touched and stroked Charlotte's pubic hair framing that small yet quite bulbous mound. She had wanted more, but he was not sure as to what to do, neither did she. He walked her home, and by the position of the moon it was late in the night now. They stood in the long grass where they had first met and kissed goodbye. Neither wanted to part, and Gillies had to promise he would return soon.

As he made his long walk home, his mind raced away with him. He understood how his parents love for each other meant so much to them. How he had loved to see Charlotte's beauty and how keen she had been to enjoy the nudity with him. His thoughts were suddenly interrupted by the calls of his father way across the valley.

He answered with his own call back in his father's direction. They kept calling at intervals until they had sight of each other. When they came into reach of each other, his father threw his arms around him and hugged him. Gillies knew from his father's face that this was just a greeting before a lecture. He was not wrong. He tried to explain why he stayed out all night, all for the sake of his new-found friend Charlotte, he stumbled around his words, and his words came out all wrong. This only added to his father's anger. Gillies suddenly realised that his father was more than unhappy about his meeting up with the outside world than just his staying out all night.

"You are far too young to be with a woman." His father said.

"But I have these feelings."

His father smiled a knowing smile. He had been his son's age once, he thought.

"Is this the place you go to when you go out with the cart and get provisions for us?"

"Yes." His father replied.

"Charlotte has spoken of her life in the town. She told me that she goes to a school there, to learn to read and write."

"You can read and write. Your mother spends many times teaching you these things."

"But Charlotte does many other things as well. She paints and makes things."

"But you have been learning more than she has. You have learned a lot from nature."

Gillies thought on this point. His father was right.

"Can I go with you to collect provisions next time?"

"We will see." His father said.

"But I want to see Charlotte again. She is very nice person."

His father sat down on a log. He patted the space on the log beside him, and Gillies sat with him. They exchanged their views and feelings about the situation. His father tried to explain that the world outside the mountain range was full of strange ways.

"Your mother and I have protected you from the evils of the outside world."

Gillies knew what his father was trying to explain, but he knew he wanted Charlotte now. He was a strong virile young man now. He felt the need to do what he had seen his mother and father do in bed, and he also knew that it was a natural thing to do. He had seen all of the animals in the forests sharing in the same way as his parents. He spoke of this to his father sitting there listening and concerned. Now it was his father that began to doubt the way they had been bringing him up, with nature being their book of life. Who wrote the rules? Gillies also knew that his freedom would be taken away from him if he ventured into the outside world. He would have to conform in many ways. His father eventually stood up and put his hand out to help Gillies to his feet. They walked with arms on each other's shoulders. His father knew that the time had come to set Gillies free to judge the world for himself.

"I'll take you with me next time I go to town."

Gillies smiled and thanked him. They came within sight of the cabin, and mother came running towards them with open arms to greet them. They were complete once again.

FIVE

For many days and nights after his venture out to meet Charlotte, he felt the urges surge through his body to make love like his parents. He ventured a few times, far enough away from the cabin so as not to be seen, so as to release these feelings and emotions; naked body arched back as his fluids spurted out high into nature's wild undergrowth. He swam the lakes to freshen up afterwards, yet his guilt remained with him when in sight of his parents. They pretended that they could not notice the changes overtaking their son now, but they were proud in seeing his development. His father would tease him about the body hair that was appearing in bushy abundance.

At night Gillies would lie in bed, his erection becoming stronger and often now. He would dream of being with Charlotte, and he just had to return to be with her again.

It was seven days since he had seen her last. He woke early that morning, walked out into the dew soaked grass a short distance away from the cabin. He was deep in thought. Just as he was about to pluck up courage to head off on the long journey to see Charlotte, his father called out to him.

"Come son. Try on some of my clothes. I am going to take you with me to town."

With his father's trousers held up by a tight belt and a baggy flannel shirt bellowing out over the trouser waist, he looked like Tom Sawyer from the books he had read.

Food was packed, with the horse and cart ready they sat together as they set off for town, with a loaded cart full of vegetables to sell at the market.

Gillies looked back and waved to his mother. Soon the cabin was out of sight, he was off to venture into the outside world. What would Charlotte think of him dressed like he was, in his father's clothes? He felt very uncomfortable and nervous in wearing clothes for the first time in his life and they felt rough against his body. He sat at his father's side on the cart in silence for most of the journey. They exchanged glances, smiled at each other. They had bumped around together on the wooden driver's seat as they headed down the rough tracks, then suddenly they were running smoothly along the main road leading into the town. Gillies began to feel nervous. He wanted to have a pee, and the cart was pulled over to the side of the road. He found a secluded spot amongst the hedgerow and wrestled with getting his penis out of the trousers; he was not used to this performance. This seemed so unnatural to him, hiding himself away in the hedge and dealing with the trousers that seemed to get in his way. As he climbed back into the cart, his father laughed and teased him for taking so long. The cart entered the town, and Gillies looked around him with amazement. He saw shops and a Church, people, some hurrying around, others just standing talking. He had seen pictures of streets like this in books, but this was for real. His father pulled on the reins and the cart stopped outside a supply shop. Gillies looked around him in the hope that he could see Charlotte. Ha, he thought. That would be a miracle.

"Come on lad, help me get the supplies." His father called up to him.

Gillies jumped down and followed his father into the shop. He stood there, amazed and a little confused. Suddenly he felt trapped and nervous, as he was amongst people for the first time in his life. At first he just wanted to run outside into the sunlight again, for this was a whole new experience for him. He felt scared. He heard his father's voice, yet his vision seemed a blur with fright. He just had to get out of the shop. Brushing past a man and almost knocking him over, he pushed the swing doors open and gasped for fresh air. He scrambled up onto the cart and sat down on the seat, not wanting to be noticed. He gasped for breath. He heard his father's voice.

"Are you alright, son?"

The cart rocked as he felt his father climb up to be at his side. A hand shook his shoulder, and he felt a little more secure now. Sweat was wiped away from his brow with the back of his hand. He turned and looked at his father, his vision returning.

"Come son, you have to face people. Be a man."

Gillies found a half smile in reply.

His father sat there for a moment, then stepped down from the cart to return to the shop. Gillies sat there for a while, and then he plucked up his courage to join him. The shop was dark inside, and it took a while for him to see and focus again. He saw sacks of wheat propped up around the walls. He looked up at the shelves to see jars of things. He had no idea what they were. His father watched him and smiled. The shop keeper reached up high to one of the jars and offered Gillies one of the contents. He looked at his father, and on seeing him nod, he reached inside the jar and took out a biscuit. He tasted it and thanked the shop keeper. As he chewed at the larger than life biscuit he judged it against the ones his mother baked in the cabin. He knew which he preferred, but thanked the shop keeper again, as it was the polite thing to do. The provisions were bought and loaded onto the cart. Gillies looked around in the hope of seeing Charlotte. He asked his father if they could find the school. The cart was driven through the high street towards the other end of the town. Gillies looked at the many faces of the towns folk, trying to imagine what it would be like living their lives in a town like that. He scratched at his chest as the shirt itched his skin.

"There. Look there is the school." His father suddenly said, pointing ahead.

Gillies stood up to look over the fencing around the school, but he couldn't see much.

His heart sank, but at the same time was glad that she couldn't see him wearing his father's clothes. The cart was turned around and they headed back along the road, into the town again. He sat on the cart while his father entered a few other shops, as he had no interest to mix with the people, they scared him. How he longed to be back in the forest now. He looked around for sight of his father, he was feeling anxious now; even Dobbin snorted and kicked the ground with one hoof. He suddenly heard his father's voice calling him. He turned to look in his direction. His father waved him to join him. Reluctantly he climbed down off the cart and joined him.

"Here lad, help me with these sacks."

Gillies bent down and took hold of one end of the first sack. His father wanted him to help him heave the sack up onto his broad shoulders. Gillies watched as his father carried the heavy load along the road and drop the sack down onto the back of the cart. On his return, Gillies was to find out that it was going to be his turn carrying the next sack. Although the load was heavy, he staggered his way along and unloaded the sack onto the cart. He looked back at his father, who stood there looking proud of his son. Gillies felt good for proving that he was that strong and becoming equal to his father. Soon they were heading back home with cart loaded with provisions. Gillies felt sad, yet in a way pleased that he had not met up with Charlotte, as he preferred to meet her as he had done in his natural state. Clothes were not for him. As the cart approached the cabin, they could see mother standing wiping her hands on her apron.

They waved to her and she started to run towards them, her face beaming smiles of happiness. Once Dobbin had been stabled and rubbed down, Gillies joined his parents in the cabin for a mug of tea. There were excited shouts of joy when his father handed her two small parcels to unwrap. She held the cotton dress against her breast and danced around the room before kissing him for the surprise gift. She then opened the second parcel which contained a sweet dress for Charlotte. Gillies smiled at the joy of the moment. His father stood there watching his sons face as he once again dipped his hand into the canvas bag and handed him a smaller package. Gillies excitedly unwrapped it, and to his joy it brandished a gleaming hunting knife and sheath. The two men hugged, as this was his father's way of accepting the fact that at last Gillies was truly a grown man now. They laughed and chatted well into the evening, but all the time Gillies was bothered by the way he had felt out of place in the town mixing with people. It was as if he had been shut in a box and not able to breathe or move freely. He knew he had been born to be free and with nature. That night in bed he just could not get the thought of being with Charlotte at the lake, and the feelings he had for her. He suddenly felt warm and wanting her. Maybe his father's gift of the hunting knife was his way of telling him that he was now ready to make his own way in life, and start to fend for himself.

SIX

A week had passed, and the thoughts of being with Charlotte again would not leave his mind. He sat at the meal table one evening, when he found himself telling his parents that he was going to go off into the mountains on his own to give himself thinking time alone. For a while there was silence around the table and he found it difficult to have eye contact with both parents.

"I think you have feelings for this young woman on your mind." His father eventually said. "You had better go and find life beyond this cabin."

Gillies looked up suddenly, not having expected this response. His mother sat there at the table, with hands supporting both sides of her face and elbows on the table. She was studying her young son with tender eyes, for now he was a young man ready to find out the facts of life for real. As parents, they had always tried to guide him through life's web of mystery through the books they had read and shared, the ways of the wild life out there in the forests and his presence at the birth of his sister. She had washed his sheets and never mentioned having sight of the tell-tale signs of youth's dreams. Now, he had to find out the final chapter of life for himself.

The morning broke and Gillies collected his new hunting knife with pride. With a slight guilt feeling, he approached his mother as she prepared food for his venture out into the wild alone. Having wrapped a large cotton cloth around chunks of cooked meat and bread, she stood there wiping her hands on her apron before taking him into her arms and clasping him to her bosom. The hug seemed to last ages before she released him. She then took his head between her hands and kissed him. He knew her thoughts were about losing her young boy and releasing him into manhood. She watched as he made his way out through the door and into the yard, he looked a fine figure of a man now, with firm buttocks and thighs so strong. She leaned on the door frame as she watched him approach his father. How alike they were now. To the outside world the scene would appear strange by seeing two naked men embrace.

"Listen my young man. You treat your young woman with respect. Remember this, she is someone's daughter. I don't agree with what you are about to do, but you are a young stag now, and well ahead of your age – you are a man now – go – go – go."

Gillies hugged his father again, turned and waved to his mother and headed out into the forest. The day was hot, and his body began to sweat with the heat of the sun bearing down on his nakedness. The words of his father were ringing in his ears, yet the thought of Charlotte and himself making love for the first time made his penis rise with anticipation. He smiled and patted it with pride as he continued to stroll towards the camp shelter that he and his father had built many months before. That night he lit a fire and ate some of the food. The stars looked brighter than normal. Maybe it was Charlotte that had lit them one by one to guide him to her. The night was colder than usual, and so he built the fire higher, and the flames danced away into the night. He heard the howl of the wolves close by, but they would not venture near him for fear of the fire. He placed his hunting knife at his side in readiness of creatures of the night.

The warm sun of the morning made him feel alive and ready for the day ahead. He ran to the lake nearby. The cool clear water refreshed his body as he dived in and swam around the rocks. The sounds of nature were all around him. He often took time out just to sit there alone listening to all the sounds. He had become quite an expert at naming the wild bird calls. The sun was rising fast now, and he knew he should move on. It was midday before he had sight of the woods that surrounded the village. He approached the long grass where he had first met Charlotte. He felt secure yet nervous as he settled down to wait for her to appear. He was not sure that he would see her this day; however, she often walked this route in the afternoon on her way home. Luck was on his side today. He heard movement in the tall grasses. He raised his head a little to see who approached. A thought ran through his head. What if it were not her, and he was caught naked like this. To his relief, there Charlotte stood, beautiful and smiling. He stood up and ran towards her. They embraced.

"Oh, my darling, how I have so wanted you," Charlotte said. 'It has been so long."

"I have missed you so much too. I have come to take you away."

Charlotte giggled then kissed him again and again.

"Will you come away with me?"

"How can I? Where would we go?"

Gillies looked into her eyes and shook his head. He had no idea, but knew they were right for each other.

"To my parent's farm, we could live in the barn and make it our home."

Charlotte giggled and wrapped her arms around him again. They could both feel their heart beats that ran faster and faster with every contact.

"Come swim with me again." Gillies begged.

Charlotte looked around her for a moment, then taking his hand, they made off towards the lake. When they were out of sight of the town area, Charlotte stopped to remove her clothes, laughing with excitement.

"There!" She shouted out. "I'm free and yours."

They reached the lake and both dived into the clear waters. Oh, how they laughed and played under the surface, with bodies entwined. They surfaced only to take another breath into their lungs before dipping below into the depths again. He felt her firm, small, yet neat breasts. She pulled his head towards them to be kissed. They swam towards the bank and climbed into the fresh green grasses and sank down out of sight from the world. Gillies lay there fondling her breasts and kissing her firm nipples. She sighed with delight and arched her back for more attention. Her hand reached down to feel his erect penis. His body quivered with the sensation of being fondled like this. What was happening to his mind and body? Never before had he been so hard. Without even a thought, he was drawn towards her pubic area. Charlotte was moist for him and he kissed and entered his tongue to taste her love juices. She cried out with joy at every thrust of his tongue. Neither of them really knew what was right or wrong in their actions. They were in love and were ready to give themselves to each other as nature would have it. They lay there panting for a while. Gillies drew a straw of new grass and ran it over her nakedness. He watched her as he rested on his elbow at her side. She wriggled, as he searched for the sensitive spots of her. He then raised his body up and knelt astride her. She took hold of his erection and guided it inside her. He shuddered at the first feeling of the entry: the warmth, the moist welcome. She raised her head and kissed him on the lips with tenderness. Then he heard her words.

"Take me darling. Take me and I will be yours."

The cries of their union of love echoed around the lake, where only the wildlife raised their alertness, and the flight of wings could be heard. Although the love act had been short, it had also been sweet and tender. They fell asleep in each other's arms, warmed by the afternoon sun. When then eventually awoke, they spoke of their love for each other. Reality came into their conversation. Many questions had no answers. There was no way Gillies plans for their future could start from this moment in time. The sun was dipping now down behind the mountains in the west. Charlotte pulled on her dress as they neared the town area. She now hated having to lose her freedom. They sat there in the long grass agreeing that the only way they could lead their lives for now was to meet like this. They were not of age where society would allow them to live as one. Charlotte began to cry. Gillies comforted her by promising her that all would be well.

He suggested that he would come out of his natural way of living and conform to her ways, if this was the only way they could be together. As he spoke, he felt a wrench in the pit of his stomach at the thought of living her ways, clothed and in a town. To his relief, Charlotte smiled, kissed him, then told him that she would only want to be with him as he was - *free with nature*. He knew that she didn't lead a happy life with her family.

SEVEN

Gillies spent the next few days deep in thought. He watched his family watching him. It was a difficult time they were going through. His parents knew that they might be reaching a stage where they would lose him, so they gave him space to work on his own problems. They had experienced the same situation back in their younger years, and they too had had to face their parents in the same way as Gillies had to do now. Gillies became moody, and his father knew that he had to confront his son so as to help release him from his torment. It was one evening as they sat at the meal table the silence was broken.

"Well, lad," his father suddenly said, "what have you decided to do with your life?"

Gillies head suddenly fuzzed up, and he was lost for words. He looked down at his plate where he had been picking at his food. His father reached out his hand across the table and took hold of Gillies hand. The grip was firm and comforting.

"Charlotte and I have found love." Gillies suddenly blurted out.

His father increased the grip of his hand and Gillies looked his father straight into his eyes. His father's look was one of understanding and not of horror as he had expected.

His mother however busied herself by doing nothing over in the far corner of the cabin. She was listening with anxious excitement, knowing well that they were about to lose a son, or gain a daughter.

"Do you really believe you have found love, or do you just believe that by Charlotte giving herself to you that means you know what love means?"

Gillies smiled.

"Well?"

"I know that in meeting Charlotte I have deep feelings for her, and would like her to be with me every day and night now."

"What about her parents then?"

"I honestly don't know her parents. They come from a different world from us. You know that, you have been to where she lives, and never once have you told me about the world out there. Why father?"

There was a long and uneasy silence as his father sat there searching for the right words to explain. Maybe he had been wrong in trying to protect his son from the evils of the outside world. He had not taken into account the fact that one day Gillies would have to be let free to make his own way in life. Was this the moment he had be dreading and trying to protect his son from. He looked across the cabin to his wife. It was as if they were as one in their thoughts. This was the moment. Dusting her apron down with her hands, a nervous habit she had when confronted with a problem, she came to sit at the table. The three of them remained silent for a while. Gillies reached out his hand towards his mother. Their hands became as one as they waited for father to speak.

"Son, life has changed in the years since you were born. Your mother and I lived a happy life here in the mountains. When you were born we had hoped that the world would be a safer place for you to grow up in. Our lives had been lived in peace. We wanted for nothing more than nature could provide for us. We had shelter, warmth, food that we grew and caught out there in the mountains. Those were happy days."

Gillies felt the gentle squeeze of his mother's hand on hearing those words. Little Charlotte stopped playing with her wooden doll and tottered across the cabin floor to the outstretched arms of Gillies. He lifted her high, and then placed her down on his lap.

Wasn't it strange the way he had helped name her at birth, and then by chance met Charlotte, the love of his life, that day across the mountain range. Little Charlotte giggled as he tickled her. She sat there as if she knew what they were talking about. Gillies realised that he might be giving up this lifestyle forever if he were to leave home and start a new life in the town. The thought of this made him feel sad.

"Well, where do we start?" father said, watching the love that was around the table now.

"I think I will ask Charlotte to arrange a meeting with you," Gillies said.

"Where and how?"

"Maybe we should meet her family halfway in the mountain range?" Mother suggested.

Both Gillies and his father nodded their approval, whilst Little Charlotte clapped her hands as in agreement. The family laughed at her antics. The tension seemed to be lifted from the situation. Father stood up and suggested that a little wine would not go amiss. The stone jar of wine tilted, and the wine flowed into the clay goblets that mother had found in the cupboard. Charlotte returned to playing with her dolls again, and mother started to prepare yet another meal. Gillies and his father sat there drinking more of the wine. Soon their serious voices changed into laughter. Mother watched her two men. How happy she was in seeing them this way. Food and more wine was consumed before the family retired to bed for the night. Gillies took time in sleeping. His mind just buzzed with excitement. How he looked forward to telling Charlotte the news that his parents were in approval of them being together. Suddenly his thoughts turned to the meeting of her parents. He had never confronted others before. The life he knew best was with his parents and the animals of the wild. He was able to talk to the animals, they seemed to understand him, but humans he was not sure about. The morning brought yet again sunlight into his room as he awoke. What would it be like waking with Charlotte at his side in bed? He lay there on his side with an arm resting across his pillow. He closed his eyes for a moment and dreamed the dream. Although he had never read about the emotions and feelings of two people in love and he had only known Charlotte for a short while, how did he understand love? Was it through seeing his parents love for each other as he grew up with them? No, that was not the total answer to the questions running through his head. He had lived in the wilds along with the animals as his friends. He had watched Bambi grow up and the way the little foal had returned to nature on his release. Yes, he had learned love through nature as well. Those feelings he had experienced with Charlotte were beautiful and exciting during their meetings in the mountains. How did he know what to do to please Charlotte? These were natural acts of love he had learned by watching the animals. But he had also seen how brutal nature could be as well. The way the Stags had locked horns in battle for place of pride over the pack. They were ruthless in their attacks on each other. Yet he had also seen the wild horses as they nosed each other in tenderness in acts of showing affection for each other prior to the act of the male mounting his mate. Then later seeing the mother giving birth to her foal, and the love and tenderness she showed in those early days of life in a harsh world out there in the mountains. He felt like a foal now. He had been shown love and he was now ready to give that love to another. He caressed the pillow and felt good about life and his future. He wanted a simple life for Charlotte and himself.

The early morning sun shone down onto his now youthful broad shoulders as he busied himself outside in the farmyard. His mother watched him as he worked, and her thoughts were mixed about what Charlotte's parents might be thinking of their lifestyle. The meeting was not something she was looking forward to. Maybe she might have to let her son go out into the world her and her husband had been trying to avoid all these years. Had they been wrong in protecting Gillies from the world?

Gillies knew this was the day he was going to trying on some of his father's clothes. He had grown into a sturdy young man now, and maybe he would fit into the clothes better this time. He smiled to himself as he remembered the last time he wore clothes on his first trip into town. How uncomfortable he had felt, and how he had been glad to get home and remove everything, and to be free again. This was the freedom he wanted. Oh God, how he hoped that Charlotte's family would agree to her living at the farm. He heard his father call him. It was time to try on his clothes. It took ages trying on the few clothes his father possessed. Mother worked wonders with her needle and cotton to take in the trousers at the waist, but the length was not worth the change as he was now nearly as tall as his father. He tried on the boots his father wore and they were a little larger than he would have liked. He stood there for his parents to amuse themselves. Although he loved to hear them laugh, he also felt uncomfortable and hurriedly removed all and stood there proud again to be naked. He was going to dread having to wear the clothes when meeting Charlotte's parents, but he had to face that day. At the crack of dawn he would head off across the mountain range to seek out Charlotte. He would carry his ill-fitting clothes in a sack, camp overnight in the forest, then the following day clamber up the slope at the end of Charlotte's town, crouch in the long grass and await her. He suddenly felt so nervous, and everything he did to kill time waiting for the sun to go down seemed to go wrong. He had been digging up potatoes from the vegetable patch and the wheelbarrow wheel snapped off as he pushed the load across rugged ground. He had collected eggs from the chickens and dropped the sack just as he was approaching the cabin door. His parents scolded him, yet they knew what nerves were running through his body. That night at bedtime there was little sleep for all in the cabin. Mother was up early making her son's food for his journey. Gillies crawled out of his bed and joined his mother. She ran her fingers through his long wavy locks of tousled hair and kissed him gently on his cheek. This was her young son in her eyes, a son she had seen grow up to be strong handsome young man. She held back a tear as she realised that she was about to let him out into the big wide world, a world she had feared about for all her life in the remote mountains.

EIGHT

Gillies watched the sun rising as he walked through the undergrowth in the direction of his camp area he had used many times now. He knew that when he reached it, he would be at the half way stage of his long trek to see Charlotte. He swung his sack full of clothes and food from shoulder to shoulder to ease the weight. Oh, how he was going to hate wearing these second-hand clothes of his father when meeting Charlotte's parents. He stopped for a while, placed the sack down on the long grass, stood there naked and free looking around. This was the spot where he had let Bambi free. Oh, how he wished he could return to those days. For nearly the first time in his life he began to feel nervous. He was pleased to reach his camp. The shelter needed some repair, so he started collecting branches and long grass to patch up the bare patches that time had eaten into. The fire soon sparked into life once he had kindled the dried fern and grass, and built up the smaller twigs. Soon he was able to place larger pieces of wood on the fire. He sat there staring into the dancing flames, and his nerves seemed to drift from his body. This was where he was at his peaceful best. He sat there as darkness fell and the stars appeared almost one by one. He loved just lying there staring up into the heavens. The shelter that night seemed to give him a sense of security. Why had he been feeling so insecure during his long trek this day? Sleep overcame him almost as soon as he placed his head down on the sack of clothes. The dream he had that night turned almost into a nightmare. There he was standing in a store in town. People were gathering around him as he stood there waiting to be served. He could feel their eyes seemed to search him from top to toe as if he was a creature from the wilds. His mind raced away, as now he was in the house of his lover's parents. The walls of the room that he and Charlotte had been given to live in seemed to be closing in on him. He stood there tearing at his clothing trying to remove these rough sack-like garments from his body to be free again. He called out into the night as he sat upright in his shelter. Sweat was pouring from his body, like flows of water from the mountains. As he ate breakfast in the early morning sunlight, his dreams flooded back through his mind time and time again. There was no way he could live in the township. He had to be free, yet he wanted Charlotte in his life. Once he had covered the fire embers with earth, he headed of once again in the direction of the town. The sun was just becoming warm now and he felt alive and happy once again to be on the move. Soon he was approaching the town. He could see across the valley to where he had first met the love of his life. How long would he have to wait in the undergrowth before she appeared? Charlotte walked daily along the same track. He lay down in the tall grass and wondered if he should put on the clothes that he was going to dread wearing. No, he would wait until Charlotte appeared. His eyes scanned the area around him. He could just see the edge of the town through the trees. The sun had now risen high; he knew that Charlotte would be appearing soon now. He lay on his back with his hands behind his head. The sun was hot on his nakedness, and soon his eyes began to close. Charlotte approached her lover with silent steps through the grass. She stood there for a while, admiring him as he slept. Drawing a sheaf of long grass, she knelt down at his side and gently touched the tip of his nose with the grass. He twitched his nose. She repeated the teasing. His hand rubbed his nose. Charlotte giggled to herself at his actions. Slowly Gillies opened his eyes.

His face lit up with a broad grin as he sat up to greet her. He pulled her down into the long grass and they kissed.

"How long have you been teasing me?" He asked.

"Long enough to know that I want you more than anything in the world."

"I'm nervous about meeting your parents." Gillies said.

They cuddled in the long grass for comfort. This was going to be a difficult day. Charlotte tugged at the sack of clothes that he had brought to wear. She laid them out so that she could see them. Her expression was amusing. Gillies looked at her.

"What do you think of them? I am going to hate having to wear them."

He stood up and struggled into the harsh sack like trousers. They felt rough against his body. With the blouse shirt now tucked into the trousers and the stout leather belt buckled to the first notch for his slim waist, he stood there for Charlotte to admire.

"You look a fine young man. Put your boots on and let me look at you."

Charlotte felt proud of her lover. He was handsome. She was sure her parents would like him. They had listened to her in the evenings as they sat there around the kitchen table. Who was this young man from the mountains? At first they listened in horror to learn about his wild living style. How could their daughter want to get married to such a young man? Did he speak well, not having had an education like Charlotte?

So many questions. Now was the day they were to meet him. They sat on the porch of their wooden house, awaiting their daughter to arrive with her young man. Francis sat on the top step watching his wife Merrill swing herself back and forth in her rocking chair. She asked him not to tap his foot so loudly. He smiled at her. They were both nervous and ill at ease now. Suddenly Merrill sat up straight and wrapped her ball of wool up, placing it in her knitting bag. Francis eyed the young man from a distance. He certainly was good looking, with almost shoulder length wavy hair. But what was he wearing? He smiled to himself as the young man looked awkward walking towards the house. He stood to greet them. Charlotte ran forward and embraced her father. Gillies stood there not quite knowing what to do.

"Father, this is Gillies."

Francis and Gillies stood for a moment in silence. Francis extended his hand for Gillies to shake. Gillies wiped his hand down the side of his trousers, he was aware that he was nervous. Their hands made contact, both were firm and strong.

"Welcome." Francis said. "Come inside. I expect you are wanting a drink after your long journey?" He said, placing a hand on Gillies shoulder. "This is my wife."

Gillies extended his hand as he was introduced to Charlotte's mother. She smiled.

"Well at last we meet. We have been hearing so many things about you.'"

Gillies felt Charlotte's hand in his as they moved towards the door that led inside the house. Gillies squeezed her hand. Thank God her parents seemed to like him. The room was dim inside, yet there was a warmth that was inviting. Charlotte guided him to the couch, and he sat at her side, not quite knowing what was going to happen next.

Charlotte's mother sat opposite them on a chair that seemed to be her personal chair, as it seemed to be sculptured for her rather roundish shape. Father returned from the kitchen parlour carrying a wooden tray with a jug of lemonade and glasses. He handed his wife a glass first, then Charlotte and turning to Gillies, the last glass was handed to him. With his own glass held forward, he gestured a toast around the room.

Charlotte smiled at her father with pride in her eyes. Her mother sat there in silence.

"Well young man. I hear you have won the heart of our daughter."

Gillies looked down at his glass, and then with a firm and positive look on his face, he nodded, then smiled at Charlotte. He then looked at her father; they smiled and raised glasses at each other again.

"Come tell us about your life up there in the mountains." Francis said as he made his way to sit in his chair.

Charlotte squeezed Gillies hand in support as Gillies coughed to clear his throat. As he began to trace his life back to as far as he could, he found that there was a genuine interest in his story. Suddenly all the fear about meeting them for this day dissolved from the pit of his stomach. He continued for what seemed ages. The only pause was for a top up of glasses by father. When he came to the meeting of Charlotte and himself he looked at her for support. She had been listening with an admiring look on her face yet had taken glances across the room at her parents. She knew that Gillies was going to be questioned. Oh, how she wished they would be kind and understanding about his life of nature. Gillies tried to describe his feelings for Charlotte. To his surprise her father spoke a few words to ease the pressure that was being placed on Gillies.

"So here you are, now wearing clothes for the first time in your life."

Gillies shook his head as he told of his visit into the town with his father that day to collect supplies. He stood up and turned his body around for his clothes to be seen. He laughed a nervous laugh as he stood there and they looked on. He told how his mother had cut and sown his father's clothes down to fit him. Charlotte laughed and tugged at his trousers, silently suggesting for him to sit down again. Gillies sat there at her side awaiting the questions.

"Don't you think you are both too young to want to get married?" mother asked.

"No." Came the quick-fire reply from Gillies.

Gillies turned to look at Charlotte. Her face was flushed now. She looked so pretty and sweet. He knew what her parents were thinking.

"I want to give Charlotte a life full of love and warmth in the mountains where peace remains untouched."

"Oh, so you want to take her away to live like you do?"

"Yes." Came another quick-fired reply.

"Where will you find the money to live?" Father questioned.

"We would make our own money from the food we grow. You see we would provide for ourselves in the same way as I have always done."

They talked well into the early evening. Question after question got answered without apology for the simplicity of each one presented. Gillies was sure that his way offered their daughter a good life.

The evening was drawing in fast now. Gillies had been offered the chance to sleep down stairs on the couch, but he felt he would be uncomfortable by being in this position. He thanked them for meeting him and making him so comfortable. He also agreed that his parents should meet with them. They all agreed that this should be at his favourite camp. Charlotte's parents watched the two of them walk off down the main road and into the distance. They had liked their daughter's choice of man to marry, but had many reservations as to how or where they were going to make their home. The thought of Charlotte being naked and living in the wildness of the mountains like that, made them doubt that this was the right start in married life for her. Gillies and Charlotte arrived at the spot where they had first met. They both felt happy about the day. Charlotte felt proud of her man and the way he had been received by her parents. Gillies and Charlotte parted, after they had sat in the long grass for a while going over the events of the day. They had agreed that the meeting of parents would be in seven days' time. They kissed, and Charlotte watched Gillies strut off into the distance. As soon as he was out of sight of the town, he removed his clothing and rolled them up and placed them back into the sack again. Oh, how good he felt being free again. The night was drawing in fast now. As he rekindled the fire, he sat there listening to the wildlife around him. This was his way of life. He was comfortable by being with nature, but he knew that to be with Charlotte, the new love of his life, he might have to live the town life. He had felt strangely uneasy. That walk through the main street, he knew that the eyes of people were on him. Yes, his clothes were the main talking point of these people, but he felt insecure as a person. Charlotte's parents had received him well and he was sure they liked him. The thought of having to live there in the town made him shudder. He threw another log onto the fire. The flame warmed him and he felt secure again. As he settled down to sleep, a fox ventured close to his shelter. Gillies smiled to himself. The fox was surely feeling as insecure as he had felt in town. He moved forward to approach the fox. The fox retreated a step, stood proud yet unsure, and then retreated into the woods. Gillies lay there, the fire keeping him warm. He had learned a lot from nature, and once again nature had spoken to him via the fox. The fox had dared to venture to into his camp, viewed the scene, made his stand for a moment, and then returned back into his own world into the wild. This is what Gillies was doing right now in his own life. He wondered what the fox was thinking. Sleep came suddenly that night. His day had exhausted him, not physically but mentally. Next morning, refreshed from a good night's sleep and with the sun on the rise, he started to break camp. As he smothered the fire with earth to deaden the embers, he was about to leave when he caught sight of the fox again. His friendly fox paused for a while as if taking stock of what was going on, and then slowly approached Gillies with caution. Gillies knelt and reached out his hand in welcome. In his mind, this was how Charlotte's father and he had been yesterday, when they met for the first time. He had been the fox. How exciting it was to learn from nature. His mind raced away to Bambi and himself and their meeting. The fox only stayed long enough to allow Gillies to stroke his head, and then he turned and quickly ran back into the woods. On that long walk back to the cabin, he had time to reflect on these events. He had taken a look at the townsfolk, like the fox had taken a look at him. The fox however had returned just to take a second look and show that his was not scared to do so. Was this a message to learn from? He had to keep an open mind if he was to love Charlotte and marry her.

NINE

There was so much to be done before the meeting of parents. Gillies' mother was in a constant state of panic at the thought of meeting Charlotte's parents. For many years now she had not ventured outside her own little world. And she could not remember the last time she had conversed with others. The family had been her life and the world out there had remained a mystery to her. Yes, she had a few items of clothing, but they had to be altered and let out as she was a little more rounded now. As for the reactions of Gillies' father, he went about his daily working in the gardens and hardly spoke. Gillies had been questioned many times about his meeting of Charlotte's parents. The nights seemed long as sleep was hard to find. Gillies' mind was full of strange thoughts about the future. He had no doubts that he loved Charlotte. He did question his emotions though. Was this love or pure sexual feelings he was having for her? Supposing after the meeting of the two families, he was destined to live with Charlotte in the town. His body began to tense at the thought of this. He suddenly woke up with his body pouring with sweat. He got out of bed trying not to disturb his parents and ran out into the night air. He ran until his lungs would not allow him to run further. He ripped handfuls of long dew soaked grass and wiped his naked body down to cool off. Back in the cabin later sitting, with his parents having breakfast, once again the conversation began to evolve around the meeting of the two families. Gillies was tense once again. His father looked sternly at him.

"What has got into you, young man?" his father asked.

"Father, I want Charlotte to live here with us. We could convert the old barn to live in.

I can't see myself living in the town."

"But supposing Charlotte does not like us or the lifestyle we live? She will surely feel strange living this way just the same as you would feel in living in the town?"

"I don't think you can decide this until our meeting." Mother said. "It's all getting too much for me to think about. If you want the barn to make into your home for her, then surely that would be fine."

Gillies looked at his father for approval. His father nodded as he drew smoke from his pipe, a pleasure he had given up a year ago, but the pressures and tensions he was now feeling had made him start smoking again. In his own mind it was not a problem as to where Gillies and Charlotte made their home, it was the meeting with Charlotte's parents that troubled him most. Gillies made his way out to the barn. He stood there in the centre of the rough floor where straw and bales of hay had been stored. He smiled to himself. He was sure Charlotte would love planning the interior with him.

The day arrived. Mother fussed around with her altered dress. She looked quite attractive as she walked around the cabin trying not to be seen as nervous. Father stood there waiting for Gillies to come down from his bedroom. Baby Charlotte tugged at her newly made dress. She could not understand why she had to wear anything at all. She kept on asking where they were going and why.

"Come on Gillies, I want Dobbin for your mother to ride on, it's a long way for her to walk for her and Baby Charlotte. Gillies appeared. He looked nervous as this was going to be the most important day in his life so far. He tugged at the belt around his waist. God, he felt uncomfortable. Dobbin was harnessed and brought out from his stable. Father helped to make his wife and Baby Charlotte comfortable for the long journey ahead. They set off with food and water for the day. The sun was kind to them, as for days now clouds had not appeared in the sky. Today however, clouds danced around the sky in thin drifts making it warm and comfortable for walking. The closer they got to the camp meeting place, the more nervous Gillies became. His mother had walked and ridden Dobbin and was tired. They arrived at the camp and Gillies showed off his talent of fire lighting. Baby Charlotte thought it great fun in collecting sticks and throwing them onto the fire. They sat and waited for their visitors.

The sun was high in the sky, which meant that it was past midday or early afternoon. Gillies was restless. Oh, how his hated having to wear his clothes. He paced up and down around the camp looking far into the distance for sight of Charlotte. His father sat watching his son. Oh, how he remembered his younger days and the pains that ran through his body when he first met Marian- his wife. Gillies suddenly saw birds in flight out of the down in the valley. Although he could not see Charlotte and her parents, the swift flight of birds were signs that there was disturbance around them. He stood with eyes straining down the valley, then suddenly his saw them. His heart jumped and missed a beat. This was the moment he had been dreading, yet knew was going to change his life. He called out to his parents that Charlotte was coming. He started running to greet them. Charlotte waved, and then suddenly they were together again. Gillies gently kissed her on the cheeks and held her hand. How strange it was that as soon as others were around they were not able to embrace and show their true feelings for each other. He shook hands with her father and was embraced by her mother. He watched her eyes as they looked him over. Holding Charlotte's hand, they approached his family and made introductions. He watched as the two fathers shook hands and the mothers eyed each other. Baby Charlotte got passed around and became the centre of attraction. Gillies' mother embraced Charlotte and smiled with approval.

At first the conversation was strained. Charlotte's parents were not comfortable having to sit down in the grass. They were not used to the outdoors like this. Gillies' parents were also feeling a little uncomfortable sitting there wearing clothes. It was quite a while before they all started to relax. Gillies was waiting for the moment when the two different lifestyles were talked about. Charlotte's mother Merrill was the first to raise the subject.

"I have to say I am a little unsure as to how feel about Charlotte living as you do."

"Oh mother." Charlotte softly said.

"Well you have to remember that you have not been brought up like Gillies."

"I quite understand what you are saying," Gillies' mother said, "but I think Gillies would find it strange living as you do also."

"That's going to be the problem we all have to come to terms with." Gillies' father said.

Gillies and Charlotte sat together holding hands, as they listened to the parents trying to plan their lives out for them. Gillies was getting inwardly more and more annoyed as to the way they were not being asked their views. He kept squeezing Charlotte's hand. As they say there in a circle on the grass, the questions bounced around between the parents. What was happening here was a questioning of Gillies' family's naked lifestyle. It was so strange a way of living. in the minds of Francis and Merrill, as they tried to understand how their daughter could want to live naked up here in the remote mountains. It was when Gillies' father suddenly turned and posed a question to the lovers. He looked at Charlotte. He had taken to her, and could see how his son was attracted to her.

"Charlotte. Let's hear what you feel about living with us as we are?" He asked.

"That's not fair, father." Gillies suddenly responded. "Charlotte will be living with me. I will be looking after her. We will have our own house and lives to live."

"I asked Charlotte." His father said firmly.

"I love Gillies, that's all I know." Charlotte said softly.

"Then why can't you both live in the town?" Her father asked.

"Because up here in the mountain we can build our own home and lives. If we live in the town, we will have to share your home, father. We want to be free."

There was silence all around. There were many questions yet to be asked. Food and drink that both families had brought seemed to break the slight tensions. Gillies was feeling frustrated. All he wanted was to be with Charlotte, but he knew there was no way he could live in the town. They sat eating the food, and the wine flowed a little, which seemed to relax the situation. Soon there were sounds of laughter even. Tales of their divided lives started to be exchanged. Charlotte's father asked the leading question. He asked how it was that Gillie's parents first decided to live alone and decided to be naked also. Gillies watched as his parents openly expressed their views about their decision to live at peace with nature. Francis, Merrill and Charlotte listened with varied expressions on their faces as the lifestyle was explained to them.

"Does that mean that Gillies has never been to school?" Francis asked

Gillies looked at his mother. She nodded. Then gestured to Gillies to answer.

"That's right. I had no need for school. We have books and my mother taught me to read and write. I didn't really know about schools and learning until I went into your town. What I do know is that Charlotte will be happy with me in our own little house." He said, as he put his arm around Charlotte. "Would you like to come and see where we would be living?"

There was a silence as they thought on this. The afternoon was drawing in now, so Gillies began to regret offering the invitation.

"So you have made your minds up as to where you are to settle down then?" Charlotte's father suggested. He looked across at his wife as if to tell her that they should give up on the idea that the young couple were going to live in the town.

"Yes, we would love to see where you intend to make your home. Thank you." Francis said, once again looking at his wife for approval.

"When can we go to see it?" Charlotte suddenly asked, realising that she had never seen it either. Giles had explained in detail what it was like, but she had never been to the farm herself. She had to face up to living with nature in the wilds of the forest. How would she feel about being naked in front of Gillies' parents? All she knew was that Gillies was the man for her. She looked at him dressed in his second-hand clothes. Oh, she liked him as she first met him, handsome, naked and strong. Oh God, how she wanted him now.

More food and drink appeared. Francis and Gillies broke away from the gathering. Gillies proudly showed off his handmade shelter. Francis was amused at what he saw. It was then that he began to realise that Gillies was a strong young man, not only physically, but in mind as well. He had warmed to the young man from their first meeting. He was tempted to lecture Gillies about how he wanted him to look after their daughter, but he knew in his own heart that he was seeing true love between them. Yes, he had doubts about Charlotte living as they did. But how could he stand in the way of love. The two families parted as they realised that the sun was lowering in the sky quite fast now. They all had long distances to walk that evening. Hugs, kisses and handshakes were exchanged by all. They had agreed to visit the cabin in the mountains in three days' time. Francis suggested that they would travel with their horse drawn buggy, and drive the long way round. Gillies gave Francis directions as the route would be the one that his father and he had taken into town. The journey home for Gillies and his parents was a happy one. They chatted and laughed over some of the difficult periods of the day. Charlotte's family were nice. Gillies asked his mother what she thought of Charlotte.

"I think you are a lucky young man to find someone like her." Was her reply.

Work continued on the farm as usual for the next couple of days. Gillies and his father toiled away on the vegetable patch. The ground had been ploughed ready for planting cabbage, onions, carrots and potatoes. Mother was busy preparing food for the visitors to be. The cabin had to be tidy, clean and just right, she kept on telling her two men. The day of the visit saw both Gillies and his father still out working on the vegetable plot, naked and sweating in the heat of the sun. They were not expecting their visitors until midday. Gillies wiped his brow with the back of his hand. He listened in disbelief as he heard the sound of the iron pan being struck. The pan was their signal that mother wanted them to return to the cabin. The sound jangled Gillies' nerves this time of hearing. He shielded his eyes against the bright sunlight and stared down the hillside in the direction of the cabin. He could just see his mother in the shadow of the cabin. In the distance though, he could see, to his horror, dust clouds rising from the dusty track leading from the far valley and up to the cabin. He called out to his father, who at the time was having a pee just off the field by the hedgerow.

"They have arrived!" He shouted aloud. "They are here."

His father finished off peeing, and shook himself, as was his usual practice. They both stood there in naked panic. There was no use in running towards the cabin as the visitors would have already arrived. Gillies suddenly found the funny side of this, but his father was not quite so amused. They started walking across the grassland towards the cabin. As they got closer, and much to their relief, mother came running towards them, carrying towels for their modesty.

"Here, wrap these around you," she giggled, "they almost caught me in the same state."

Charlotte and her parents were standing outside the cabin as the two men, with their towels wrapped around them, approached them, looking a little sheepish. Charlotte was laughing at the sight. She ran towards Gillies and kissed him, tugging at his towel as she teased him. They all greeted each other, there was much laughter.

Charlotte's mother seemed a little embarrassed, but soon saw the funny side of the situation. Tea was made ready, and they all sat around chatting. Gillies and Charlotte left the parents so as to allow Gillies to show her the barn that they would make into their home. Charlotte was excited as she skipped around making suggestions as to what would go where. They were joined by her parents. Her mother seemed a little doubtful about Gillies' ideas. Although she liked him, she had doubts in her head about what the future would be like for her daughter. To her the lifestyle seemed far from what she had in mind for Charlotte. As the day progressed though, she could see that Charlotte was so in love with Gillies, and the family seemed to have found a way of life that in a way she was beginning to understand. Her own life had been township, born and bred. She had listened to answers posed to Gillies' parents about how and why they had chosen to detach themselves from the world outside. They for sure had been able to provide for themselves. They had also produced and brought up a lovely young man. But the world was still changing. The talking continued through the day. Gillies' parents had seen a secure way of living when they were Charlotte's age. How could she stand in her way? Who was right, and who was wrong? Charlotte and her parents walked around the vast area in the mountainside talking. They talked and discussed, doubted yes, but started to understand Charlotte's choice, not only in Gillies, but his lifestyle. Gillies sat with his parents waiting for Charlotte's return, nervously wondering what Charlotte's family would want for her. The final cup of tea of the day was made and the summing up of the day came from Charlotte's father.

"Well thank you for inviting us into to your lovely home. We can't quite understand why Charlotte would want to marry Gillies here, but we can now understand her wanting to live your way of life. Therefore, young man," he said, turning to Gillies, "we give our approval of you both getting married. May nature's God bless you both."

Gillies let out a sigh of relief, and in his excitement, he jumped up from the stool he had been sitting on to embrace Francis and shake his hand. In his haste, he forgot he still had the towel draped over him. As he lurched forward, the towel unravelled and fell to the floor, exposing him. He suddenly tried to cover himself again, but too late.

"Well I was not expecting that." Francis said. "Maybe you are preparing us for when we visit you after your marriage."

Laugher saved the day and embarrassed blushes of Gillies.

Gillies recovered his dignity and embraced everyone. Charlotte hugged her parents, and as she was about to embrace Gillies' mother she suddenly felt that at last her world was beginning to become alive. The warmth of her embrace was more than she had expected. Gillies, on seeing this, hurried across the room and the three of them hugged together with tears of joy. Charlotte's parents called out to her to get ready for their journey home. Gillies and his parents waved goodbye to their visitors as they made their way back down the dusty track and away down the valley and into the distance.

Gillies sat that evening with his parents talking over the days visit. His parents had taken a liking to Charlotte. There was much work to be done on the barn in the next six months before the wedding date. It had been planned for Gillies' eighteenth birthday.

TEN

After Charlotte's family had left, Gillies sat there that evening with his parents chatting over the events of the day. They had taken Charlotte into their hearts. He had expected to be questioned about many things, things that were maybe personal to him. But to his relief they didn't. Once in bed, he listened to their voices as they drifted up from their bed below. It was obvious that they had worries about how Charlotte would deal with being part of their way of life. His own head was full of thoughts, some good, some doubts. What was happening to his life? He had grown up in the wilds of the mountains knowing only of nature's ways of life. He had not mixed with others, and his only friends had been the animals of the wilds. Now that he had met his lover, Charlotte, was his life about to change? Listening again he strained to overhear the conversation of his parents, downstairs in bed. They were discussing and wondering if he had had sex with Charlotte before marriage. Although he heard their words, he had also questioned his own actions. Surely if he was in love with Charlotte then to make love to her was not wrong. His thoughts rushed back to their first love act. How beautiful and wonderful that moment had been. Although he had not studied at school, he had learned about life through nature, and had watched the stag defending his territory. He smiled to himself as this was his father's role in the family. His father had decided to stake his claim to freedom when he had married his mother. Now he was about to repeat history with Charlotte. With the thoughts of how he would work on the barn to make a home for Charlotte, sleep overtook him.

The weeks that were to follow saw his work on the barn, the work on the farm, plus shooting and fishing for food, kept well occupied. His desire to see Charlotte again became stronger and he just had to meet her again. His parents were not sure that the delay in their son's marriage was wise. He was a young healthy young man and acting like a young stag at times. When they were approached by Gillies about going away for a few days up into the mountains, they knew what his intentions were. Morally they were opposed to this, yet they knew that they could do nothing to change his mind. The morning that he left for the wild of the mountains he still found that his mother had packed much larger packs of food than usual. His parents watched as he set off. His strong sturdy youthful young body made them feel proud of him. How he reminded his mother of what her young husband had looked like in those years. The difference was that they had met as a couple in the township. Clothes were discarded once they had agreed to live with nature and provide for themselves from the land. They were divinely happy to escape from conventional life. They became free, and when Gillies was born, they continued that way of life. Now that Gillies had grown up only knowing the rules of nature, they were beginning to challenge their own views and way of life. Had they been right in protecting their son from the outside world? They hugged each other as they stood in the doorway of the cabin watching Gillies' strong naked body wander off across the fields of lush green grass. Soon he had gone out of view. They knew that he would be safe out there in the wilds, but they were not sure that Charlotte was going to be able to understand the future in front of her. They had preached the way of nature to Gillies, and now they had to trust that they had done the right thing. Gillies camped the night, alone with his thoughts. The fire crackled away as the night sky lost its heat from the sun. He felt free and happy to be out there again. He unwrapped the food his mother had prepared, and drank the wine his father had added to his bag. The clothes that his had brought along with him this time were laid out to help the creases smooth out. Oh, how he hated the thought of wearing clothes again in the town. He suddenly remembered the fox that had ventured into his camp area last visit. What was that lesson from that visit? He laughed to himself as he remembered. The fox had appeared, checked him out, and then returned into the wild again. It was like his trip was going to be this time to see Charlotte. He would walk into town proud to be who he was. Yes, he would conform to the ways of the town folk were. No, he could not match them for the clothes they wore, but he was a better man than any of them under them. So he, like the fox, would walk tall and return to his own way of life when he was ready to do so. He slept with those thoughts in his head. He curled up under the shelter and slept soundly that night. The way in which he and his father had constructed the shelter let the early morning sun to enter and warm him. He lay there on his back as he teased his early morning erection. What was it that made a man have these feelings? He sat up scratching his pubic hair as usual. How he loved his freedom.

He listened to the world of nature around him. This was one of the many things that the town folk would not have enjoyed. His ear was tuned to the sounds around him. Nature talks to people and can be heard by those that choose to hear. To his delight, the fox appeared. Gillies sat there quite still as this friend appeared. Gillies reached out his hand gently. The fox stared for a moment, unsure, yet not afraid. Gillies reached into his food bag and fumbled for an offering. He held the small piece of chicken meat in his hand and offered it to the fox. They both remained still for a moment. The front paw of the fox stretched forward, like a wild cat does when stalking its prey. Gillies offered the meat, and the fox took it quickly, stood there for a moment, and then ran off back into the wooded area. Gillies was happy to have his friend visiting him again. The water of the natural lake was warm as Gillies swam around and bathed his body clean from his journey of the day before. He looked around to see if his friendly fox was to be seen, but no. He laid out on the rock and the edge of the lake to be dried by the sun which was getting quite hot now. It was time for him to finish the second stage of his journey. With the ashes of the fire well covered with earth, he set off in the direction of the town. The sun was high in the blue sky when he approached the town. He stood in the long grass to dress into his clothes. He hopped and stumbled as he tried to get one leg into his trousers. Oh, how he hated this rough material against his body. The shirt was slipped over his head, and he ran his fingers through his hair. Taking a deep breath, he continued his journey into the town. He was aware that people were giving him glances, and some even stared at him as he walked along the unmade road, but he walked tall and proud, as the fox had done. At one stage, he stopped and stared back at a small group of young lads. None of them spoke or called out, but just stared. His returned stare made them unsure of him, and they strolled off down the road. Soon he was approaching Charlotte's house. It was a wooden house painted white. It had a porch and three wooden steps leading up to the front door. He stood there for a moment, collecting himself. He told himself not to be scared or frightened of townsfolk. They were unsure of him, so he had the advantage. He knocked on the front door and waited. He coughed and cleared his throat. Yes, he was nervous now. He could hear footsteps from inside the house. Suddenly the door was opened.

Charlotte's mother Merrill stood there for a moment before speaking.

"Well, look who we have here." She said, smiling and reaching out her arms to welcome him. 'Come in. I will call Charlotte downstairs. She has been cleaning her bedroom. How are your parents?"

"They are fine, thank you." Gillies said, his voice sounding a little high pitched.

"Charlotte. Gillies is here. Do you want to see him?"

Gillies watched Merrill as she tidied the couch of needlework for him to sit down on. He liked her, and hoped that the feeling was mutual. Merrill disappeared out into the back of the house, leaving him to look around. He wandered around, looking at the pictures framed in dark wood. They all seemed dull in the dimly lit room. He was attracted to the large bookshelves that ran along one wall. He squinted his eyes to read the titles. Somehow his eyes seemed to blur. Must be nerves he thought. Not knowing his books that well, he just picked one out of the stack. He sat down to read. Where was Charlotte? What was she doing? He was just about to start to read when Merrill returned with a tray of what turned out to be lemonade. He looked up from the book as his realised that his was being offered a glass.

"Lemonade?" Merrill asked.

"Thank you."

"So, you can read well?"

Gillies looked a little embarrassed at the question.

"Yes. My mother taught me to read. I think I was about three when I could read my first book. It had a lot of drawings, so it helped." He laughed.

"Oh, that's nice. Did you never want to go to school?"

"I never knew there were schools, until I came into town here with my father."

Merrill shook her head, tutted, and then called upstairs to Charlotte again. Gillies could hear hurried footsteps across the floor upstairs. He looked down at his book again, not quite knowing what to say to break the silence that had now come about. Merrill once again went out to the back room. Suddenly Charlotte appeared. Gillies smiled and stood to greet her. They embraced and kissed. Gillies twirled her around to look at her. She looked beautiful, and told her so. She blushed and kissed him again.

"I didn't know you were coming to see me."

"I couldn't stay away. I really can't wait for my birthday to come around."

"How is the barn looking?"

Gillies sat her down on the couch and told her how he had worked hard, and how nice and clean it looked. He loved the feel of her body close to his own, but how he wished that she was not wearing clothes as the body contact was far more exciting. Merrill entered the room again. She looked at the two lovers, smiled and remembered her courting days. But this was different. Charlotte had found Gillies, a young man from the mountains. A young man that had never been to school or worn clothes in his life. Many an hour she had spoken with Francis about Gillies' family life. And although they would have liked her to have married a young man from the town, they could not fault Gillies. They also realised that if this was their daughter's wish to live Gillies' way of life, then they should try to understand her wishes, or maybe make her unhappy with a man of their choosing. When Francis arrived home for the evening meal, Gillies began to feel a little uncomfortable. He was sure that he was going to be invited to stay the night. He was not used to living the way Charlotte's family did. Where was he going to sleep? Should he sleep in his clothes? Many questions ran though his head as he watched the table being laid. Charlotte reached out and took hold of his hand to squeeze it. Gillies hand was feeling sweaty. She knew she had to try and protect him from the pressure he was feeling. She also knew that there was no way they could make their marriage work if they were going to have to live in the town. They both wanted to be free from the pressure of daily life of town folk.

"Come on you two, up to the table and eat up." Merrill said.

Gillies looked at the way the table was laid. He was not used to seeing so many knives, forks and spoons. A bowl of soup was placed in front of him. He nervously watched and waited to see which spoon was to be used by Charlotte. She smiled across the table at him and reached out for her own soup spoon to show him. Gillies stretched out his foot under the table, and Charlotte's foot made contact. They smiled at each other across the table and Gillies started to relax a little. The conversation was a little tense at first, but soon livened up. The questions seemed to be directed at Gillies way of life. He could see how Merrill was just unsure as to how Charlotte would adapt to the nude lifestyle. She could not understand how Charlotte, having been brought up in a community where schooling and church teaching had been strict, could suddenly want to lead the life of Gillies' family. Gillies suddenly found his voice and confidence. Merrill and Francis sat there in total silence as they listened.

"My parents, before they had me, decided that they wanted to be free of a troubled world where values of life demanded conforming to others ruling. There were many things that they did not agree with. They were educated and church going folk, but they disagreed with too many issues. They were so in love, and these restrictions and the greed of money, material things and values brought strain on their lives. Their love for each other was stronger than the world out there as they saw it. They claimed their land after payment of deeds, built their farmhouse, toiled the land and grew their own vegetables. I came along, and my father taught me to hunt and fish in the wild. They need for nothing, and are more in love, not only with each other, but with their lifestyle. I know that I can make Charlotte happy living this way."

He sat there, not really believing he had been confident enough to express himself so well. He looked at the faces of Merrill and Francis. There was silence for a moment.

"Well my young man, you have made you case clear to us. Thank you," Francis said.

Charlotte looked happy and proud about her lover. They sat around the fire later that evening chatting about the wedding. Charlotte's parents would make arrangements with the church, and they would keep the reception simple. Gillies listened, and all the time had visions of how his parents would deal with this return to the outside world. How his mother would fuss over what she would wear for the day. Gillies sat looking into the flames of the log fire as the conversation continued to evolve around his future. Suddenly his head nodded forward onto his chest. Charlotte laughed at the way he tried to hide the fact that he felt tired. Francis, on seeing this, got up out of his chair and disappeared out of the room. On his return, he carried a canvas type bed. He opened up the wooden struts that formed the legs of the bed. He placed it over in the far side of the living room. Merrill gathered some blankets and prepared a bed for Gillies to sleep in. Charlotte placed her arm around Gillies shoulders as she leaned forward to whisper in his ear.

"There you are, bedtime for my man."

Gillies smiled as her parents headed upstairs to their own beds. Merrill had kissed him on his cheek as she handed him a striped night shirt. Gillies thanked her. He had never worn a night shirt before. As he striped to the waist to wash at the kitchen sink, he felt Charlotte's arms caress him from behind. He was slightly nervous as her parents had only just gone into their own bedroom. Surely he couldn't show his love for Charlotte with her parents listening to their every move. Charlotte giggled at his resistance. Her hands searched for his nipples. She knew his weaknesses already from the times they had swam together in the lake. Oh, how he had been aroused as they made love on the rocks in the middle the lake.

"Charlotte darling, please don't tease me like this."

He turned to face her. Their bodies made contact, and Charlotte could feel his erection pushing into her crotch. How she writhed on this. She looked into his eyes, they were dreamy and half closed with desire. Her hand reached down to take hold of her man's pride and joy. He moaned approval. He leaned back against the stone sink as he felt her hand undo the buttons of his trousers. Her hand slipped inside and took hold of his erection. The act was far too exciting to resist. He leaned back and let her take him in her hands. His trousers dropped down around his ankles. He was just about step out of them when he heard movement from upstairs. He panicked, and quickly bent down tried to retrieve his trousers. He heard the door open up stairs.

"Charlotte. I think I would like to see you in your own bed now. You will soon have many times together." Her father called out.

Charlotte kissed Gillies hurriedly, leaving him erect and frustrated in his nudity. She waved and smiled as she made her way upstairs. Oh, what a beautiful body her man had, she thought. Having washed under the cold water that he had pumped up into the sink, he unfolded his nightshirt and held it against his body. It was long and reached down to the floor. He pulled it over his head and let it unfold down his body. He caught sight of himself in the mirror that hung on the back of the door. He looked stupid. He stood there for a moment smiling at the sight. He sat on the side of the makeshift bed and tried to master the art of getting in between the blankets without his nightshirt riding up his body. As he pulled the blanket up around him, the nightshirt rose as well. It took a while to master the art of this, but by the time he had, his eyes were fast in closing. It was a very short sleep, as he wrestled for ages with the nightshirt; he had always slept naked and free. This was pure torture for him. Throwing back his blankets, he tugged at his nightshirt, removed it and threw it across a chair. He climbed back into bed and sleep came instantly. The next thing he knew was that his nose itched. He reached out to scratch it. Opening one eye just a little, he squinted through the haze of early morning waking. There was a shadow shielded him from the light. He eased himself up onto his elbow. It was Charlotte standing there waving the nightshirt in his face. She laughed and giggled at his antics. Kneeling down at the side of his bed, she laid herself across his chest, and he embraced her. He tried to encourage her into his bed, but that was impossible as it was just about strong enough to hold his own weight. To his surprise and delight she went down on him. He moaned his approval as she kissed his erection. He stretched his arms high above his head in sheer delight of being seduced this way. How natural it all seemed. The sound of movements upstairs soon brought the pair of them back to reality. Charlotte dashed into the kitchen and made kitchen noises, such as water being pumped up to fill the kettle. Gillies hurriedly pulled himself into the nightshirt and returned to bed. By the time Charlotte's parents arrived downstairs, he had sorted his nightshirt out. He wished them 'good morning' in a sleepy fashion. He knew what they were thinking.

The morning went quickly once breakfast was over. He had managed to get dressed and washed without being observed. It felt so unnatural being with others around him as he tried to hide his embarrassment. So when it came time for him to head off home to his cabin life, he was relieved. Charlotte walked with him to the end of town. Gillies had thanked her parents for having him stay overnight. They passed the church where soon their marriage would take place. It was going to be a small service. They had agreed that last night. How Gillies dreaded the thought of that day. He told Charlotte of his fears and she laughed and hugged him for being that way. It was going to be a happy day. They reached the place where they had first met. The sun was now high in the blue sky now as it had been on their first meeting. They laughed about that special day in their lives, when the boy from nature, met the town girl. The journey back home for Gillies was full of thoughts. He remembered Bambi. The first time he saw dears mating in the wild of the mountainside. Then there was the first time he had seen his parents making love in bed, and the birth of his little sister. Life was wonderful, and nature offered many answers to life's mysteries. He had never come into contact with people before that visit into town with his father that day. For sure he had never had contact with a female before meeting Charlotte. How natural were the feelings that had ran through his body on feeling that first touch to his body as they first fumbled for their first kiss. How do babies learn words to speak? How is it that when two people meet, that message of love can send a feeling of excitement through your body? He smiled at his thoughts. Now out of sight of the town, he removed his clothes and felt the warmth of the sun on his naked body again. How lucky he was to have been brought up living with nature.

He reached his half-way camp. The sun was sinking fast. He lit a fire, and reached for the rope that held his food in a sack high up from the ground. He lowered the sack down; it had not been attacked by wildlife. As he sat there eating, he listened to the wild life out there in the woods. His friend the fox called to check him out and carried away a piece of chicken that Gillies offered him. He had earned the trust of his friendly fox. From the short time he had spent in the company of the town's people, he began to wonder if he would find people to trust like he did with animals. There were many things on his mind when he tried to sleep. The night was hot, so he wandered through the woodland to the lake. The cool water was welcome. He slipped his body into the water rather than disturbing the wildlife if he had dived in the water. He swam to the rock out in the middle of the lake where he had made love to Charlotte. The moon was bright and shone across the lake like a lighted torch. He watched his own refection in the water, and wondered if sometime in the future he would have a son that he could teach the wonders and beauty of nature. Surprisingly, he slept there out on the rock until the early morning light. Swimming back to the lakeside refreshed him for his second half of the journey home. With the fire embers covered with earth, he headed off. He saw his friend the fox appear for a moment from out of the long grass, he waved to him, as he scurried off back into the wild.

His parents were working and could not be seen as he approached the farmhouse. Suddenly he caught sight of Little Charlotte. She stood there for a moment not believing that her brother was home again. She started running towards him with arms outstretched, her shouts of joy being heard by his parents. Gillies picked Little Charlotte up in his arms, raised her up so that she sat on his shoulders. She giggled as she ruffled his hair all over his face. His mother greeted him with a kiss, and his father appeared from the tool shed.

That evening he was bombarded with questions until time for bed. His parents were full of questioning their own decision to live their lives away from society as they saw it when they got married. Had they been selfish in bringing Gillies into the world and isolating him from people? At the same time, they felt proud that their son had grown up in the wild learning life through nature, and not from the minds and lack of morals of the society they were living in when he was born. Now, for the first time in Gillies life, he was about to have to conform to the laws of society by getting married to Charlotte. Why? That was the burning question in their minds. Then their thoughts were with Charlotte. Was it by falling in love with Gillies, she was rebelling against the life she had been brought up to know, and conform to? Only time would answer these questions. Nature, and the freedom it had given them, was Charlotte now seeing this in the same way as they had, when they escaped into the wilds of the mountains to find the meaning of life through nature. The church where the marriage was to take place was seen by the town's folk as the place to commune with God. These same people would be closer to their God if they communed with their God in the natural surroundings of nature. For them, nature produced food for their table and enough vegetables to sell if they needed money for just the bare essentials for their merger lifestyle. With these thoughts, they were happy now with their lot.

ELEVEN

The Wedding

Gillies and his parents had attended the wedding rehearsal. He had been introduced to Daniel, a young friend of Charlotte's. He came from Holland, and was to be the best man. Gillies was nervous throughout the short ceremony. The priest stood there in the church looking down on the young couple getting married. From the outset, it was obvious that he did not approve of Gillies as he was not of the townsfolk. Charlotte's family were regular attenders of the church and so Gillies was accepted on those grounds. Daniel had been great. He had guided Gillies through the routine and got him to repeat the vows over and over again, but when it came to the time of repeating these in front of the priest, his words would not leave his mouth. Charlotte squeezed his hand several times to reassure him that all would be fine on the day. As Gillies and family were on their way home, they remained silent as their cart rattled down the main high street. Eyes seemed be all on them. Gillies had seen the same group of youths standing there smiling and talking in whispers, as the family from the wilds passed them.

His first reaction was to leap down from the cart and confront them. His father, seeing his anger, took hold of his arm to restrain him.

"Gillies, you have to allow them to not understand."

"But I want them to understand." Gillies said, tugging his arm free.

"Then you do that not by force, but by example. Why do you think your mother and I made our stand in life?"

"And are you happy that you did that?"

There was a silence between them for a while before his father attempted to reply.

"Well son, Charlotte has seen life as it is in the town."

"What are you saying?"

"I'm saying, Charlotte found you, and through that, has seen how you live daily. She is giving up her life in the town to be with you. She is giving up all the things she has grown up with to live with you and nature."

The cart came to rest. They were all home again. To the world outside, the sight of them all removing their clothing as soon as they entered the farmhouse would have seemed strange, but this was the freedom they had strived for. The way townsfolk hid their true identity with fashionable clothing seemed equally strange to them. Gillies' father's words rang in his head. Charlotte had seen their way of life, compared this with her own upbringing, and made her choice. He was not sure if his love for her would have lasted, if he had been forced to live in the town with her. These thoughts echoed through his mind as he busied himself in putting the finishing touches to the converted barn. The final stage was to remove his own bed from the farmhouse into the barn. This would leave his bedroom up in the loft space free for his little sister to have for her own. There was an air of excitement as Little Charlotte gathered her dolls up ready for the move. The day of the wedding was fast approaching. Gillies and his father worked hard out there in the vegetable gardens, and the hunting and fishing continued as usual. The question of love making was never a problem. Gillies had learned the facts of life the natural way by watching the animals of the wild mating. The only doubt Gillies had, was how to control babies being born each time they made love. It was when he and his father were taking a rest to take food and drink in the fields, when the question was posed to his father.

His father sipped at his wine from his stone jug for a moment. He paused for thought.

"Well my young man, you will have to learn how to control yourself. It's not easy at first, but you will learn that just as you are about to ejaculate, you have to withdraw."

Gillies laughed at the thought. He dare not tell his father that he had not done that act with Charlotte when they first met. He had seen the deer mating. The stag and master of the herd had not withdrawn. He questioned this act with his father.

"Well, they only have acts of sex once a year. Think on that, son."

They both sat there for a while before laughter overtook them. Gillies felt good that he and his father were able to talk about this so naturally. He also felt so lucky that he had learned about life through watching and learning, through living with nature.

The night before the wedding, Gillies and his father moved his heavy double bed from the farmhouse and carried it into the now converted barn. Gillies stood there looking around the home he had built. He hoped that Charlotte would like her new home, he was sure she would, as it was bright and clean. There were logs at the side of the fire, and outside there was stacked high more logs that he had chopped. He smiled to himself as he felt the muscles in his arms. He had also made a trestle table and two stools. His parents had given them two fireside chairs and many oddments that he would never have thought of. They were set up for their new way of life. He was soon to be the master of his own house. He smiled again at his own thoughts. As he walked back to the farmhouse, Little Charlotte came running out begging him to look at her new bedroom. He picked her up in his arms and kissed her. She hugged him for letting her have her own room. He watched her as she struggled to climb the crude wooden ladder that rested against the loft floor. He followed her. She excitedly jumped up onto her bed and begged him to sit at her side. He cuddled her and tickled her. The cries for help echoed around the farmhouse. She loved her brother. As the family sat around the log fire that evening, there was an air of calmness as they reflected back on their past years there.

It was the eve of the wedding day. Gillies decided to sleep down stairs on the floor of the farmhouse. He knew he wasn't in for a good night's sleep anyway, and so he might as well just lay there with blanket pulled over him for warmth. Next morning, the day of his wedding, he woke having slept much better than expected. Over the past few months, he had invented all sorts of problems in his mind as to how this day was going to make him so nervous, but he felt good and ready to face the world. He stood outside the farmhouse under the cold water shower. The sun was already warm. He felt alive and happy. His thoughts were for the wedding night. They were not going to spend their wedding night in their new home. They had planned to stay in the shelter up in the mountain where they first made love. He felt the first signs of an erection coming on as he remembered how beautiful that day had been, but restrained himself of the temptation. There seemed to be panic between his parents as they prepared themselves for the day ahead. His mother was nervously trying to get dressed but nothing seemed to be going well. His father was ironing his shirt for the second time. Gillies watched this scene as he pulled his trousers on and tucked his shirt inside. How he hated clothes. They set off early, as the journey was going to take a while. Gillies sat with his little sister in the rear of the cart with legs swinging over the edge as they sang songs that their mother had taught them. Little Charlotte was curious about the sack of food that mother had prepared for the newlyweds. Little Charlotte wanted to see the goodies inside the sack. Gillies continually teased her by looking in the sack and pretending to take food out and smuggle it into his mouth. The sun was high in the sky as they approached the town. The townsfolk had gathered outside the church in curious mood. Who were these strange people from the mountains? The cart drew up at the wall of the church, and Dobbin was tethered. Gillies helped Little Charlotte down from the cart. She wanted to hold onto his hand as if to say, 'please don't leave me'. Daniel, the best man, was there to greet them. He greeted them with a handshake and a smile. There were very few attending the service, but as Gillies and Daniel walked down the short aisle, Gillies was suddenly aware that his legs were not as steady as normal. He was pleased to sit down with Daniel at his side on the front row of seats, to await the arrival of Charlotte. His vision seemed blurred as he tried to look around the church. He felt sick and heady as he sat there. The priest took up his position just a few paces away from Gillies. His face was bland and red. He looked very stern and was not wanting to look in the direction of Gillies. Gillies just wanted to get up and run away into the mountains, a world he knew, and was comfortable in. Panic was beginning to take his body over, but at the point of giving into the feeling, the sound of music from the small little organ hidden out of sight at the back of the church was heard. The sound of the off-key music heralded the arrival of the bride.

Daniel nudged Gillies in the ribs. They stood up to face the priest. Gillies felt sick with nerves, but the sight of Charlotte seemed to calm him. She looked beautiful dressed in a simple spring looking dress, and carrying a posy of white daisies. They exchanged glances, and the priest brought them together in the aisle in front of him. Gillies felt nervous as the ceremony started. All he wanted was to let these words that were being said by the priest pass through his head speedily before he was sick with nerves. He felt Charlotte's hand reach out for his to comfort him. His own hand was wet with nervousness. He faintly heard the words of the priest who was asking him to repeat the vows. Daniel passed a ring over to him, and it was all he could do to place the ring on Charlotte's finger through shaking hands. Once the vows were said, the register had to be signed. This to him was a piece of paper where with the priest's finger pointed the space as to where he had to put his name. Yes, he had learned to sign his name, yet somehow the ink loaded pen would not function. His signature was not the one he had practised so often in the peace of the farmhouse. The priest hastened the closing of the book. The organ played again, and the small group of people, which had been a blur to Gillies, made their way out of the church and into the fresh air again. There were tears and kisses being shared around. The two families were now as one on record. Gillies often challenged this point in his own mind, for he only wanted Charlotte, to love and protect. Yes, he had a God, but surely God was out there in nature. God was all around, so why did he have to go to a wooden church to repeat words of a priest? Words that were meaningless. Surely God would know his intentions were honourable. Did the stags out in the wilds of the mountains, when choosing their mate have to attend a church? He smiled at his own thoughts. He was at last coming to terms with the day. He walked Charlotte back to her parents' house for the last time. They drank wine and ate food that had been prepared, listened to words of wisdom, received many kisses before they left to make their love recorded for all time in their own way. They turned and waved to their families as they headed out of town and towards the mountains in the distance. There were curtains in windows flickering as they passed a few houses, and there were glances of interest from the verandas and porches where townsfolk sat watching the passing day. They waved back to the few people that called out good luck to them. They must have seemed a strange couple to most onlookers, but for them this was the beginning of a new life.

Soon they were alone in the green pastures that led to the foot of the mountains. Only then did they feel free and as one. They laughed as they removed their clothes and bundled together to place on the pack Gillies was carrying. Now, naked and free, they lay down in the green grass and kissed with passion. They lay there for ages just caressing each other's bodies, as if to find if they were really together at last. The sun was slowly going down in the west as they reached the woodland of the mountainside. Their walking pace seemed to have quickened. There was an air of excitement as they reached their camping area. The shelter was still standing and needed only a little attention. With the fire now sparking into life, they squatted down crossed leg and naked. They had pre- planned this for many months prior to the wedding day. They sat there for a while facing each other, knees touching and hands outstretched to hold. They looked into each other's eyes, leaned forward and gently kissed. Gillies cleared his throat to find his true voice, his voice he had failed to find in the church. They then looked to the heavens as they spoke the words they had rehearsed in secret.

"Please God; bless us in our life ahead. May you bless our love, and let nature guide us in all we do."

They sat for a while in silence. These were simple words shared with God's nature. Words that they felt were all that was required to be said to bond them as one. Nature was their world from now on, they felt lucky to have found each other's love through nature. This night was to be a night of pure love as they lay there in each other's arms, warm and secure in their new life. Their lips touched and tongues danced. Gillies fondled Charlotte's firm breasts, her nipples stood proud. His tongue touched the tips and her body writhed with joy. Her hand held his erection and encouraged it to an even greater strength, for she wanted him so badly now that he was hers. Her lips parted and sucked just the head of his shaft. He moaned in approval as she took him in deeper. He fondled her crotch, so warm and moist now with desire. He eased his body over hers, and entered her with such understanding and care. That first entry brought a cry of joy that echoed around their encampment. She arched herself as his hands held her buttocks so firm, so beautiful, as he entered her deeper with firm thrusts. His head looked to the sky as he pulled her towards him with her pubic hair so wet with the joy of love. The fire flickered its light across their naked bodies that were entwined with love. Gillies withdrew, his love juices spread high across his lover's body. They laughed at the love that they had just made. They lay at each other's side, both admiring the others nakedness. Charlotte, her body so smooth with the young and beautiful roundness of a nymph, her breasts were firm yet not large, just beautiful. The mound covered with bushy pubic hair seemed to stand proud and wanting. Gillies ran a finger through the remaining love juices that nestled there. He looked at her and smiled. She in turn placed her hand across his chest and finger teased his nipples. He moaned his approval. They were exploring each other's desires and wants. They wanted to please. Her hand ventured down to his now flaccid penis. Slowly it became alive in her hand. She looked into his eyes for approval. He laughed a little at her rather clumsy way of handling his pride.

He guided her hand so as to hold in it a way that would please him most. He had since that first time of making love to himself, found by trial and error the most exciting hold. Charlotte slapped his hand after he had shown her, then set about pleasing him his way. They moved into the shelter for the night. Gillies felt the chemistry running through his body as they lay curled up together. Yes, there was an awakening during the night, but sleep called as it had been quite a day in all. The morning light brought sunlight streaming into the shelter. Gillies looked at his wife, she was beautiful laying there. He carefully removed his arm from around under her, then went and rekindled the fire. He then wandered off into the fringes of the woodland, where the early morning dew felt good beneath his feet. He searched to find daisies amongst the wild flowers. There he found them, almost in a clump together as if waiting to picked by him. As he sat there by the fire cooking breakfast, Charlotte awoke. She rubbed her eyes with the back of her hands. She yawned, and Gillies crawled to her side. He kissed her on the lips. She was trying to find her bearings. As she began to sit up, she felt the daisy that he had placed in her navel move. She took hold of it in her hand and placed it against her lips. She kissed the daisy, and then placed it against Gillies lips.

"Thank you my darling, that was sweet," she said, her face blooming with joy,' I am going to press that in a book when we are at home."

Gillies smiled. He knew that Charlotte was about to learn about the simpler things of life living with nature. He knew she was going to be happy. Later that morning they swam again in the lake. They teased and called out aloud to each other. Their voices echoed around the lake, and return to them. They were alone in the world together in love. They made passionate love on the rock that stood proud in the centre of the lake. It was as if it had been placed there for love making. As they lay there after making love, looking up into the blue still skies, Gillies wondered if they were the first ones to make love on this rock. He stood up tall and proud, legs apart and with folded arms. Charlotte looked on in amusement as he announced to the world.

"I claim this rock, and name it, *Young Charlotte's Rock.*"

Charlotte sat up and wrapped her arms around his firm legs. She was so proud of him.

With the camp area cleared, and the burning embers of the fire covered with earth, they stood there for a moment in silence. This place would always remain special in their hearts. With one last glance back, they headed towards their new home across the valley and up into the mountains. As they approached the farmhouse, Little Charlotte was the first to see them. She came running towards them. Her face beamed with joy. Gillies put down the heavy sack that carried clothes and cooking utensils. Little Charlotte rushed into his arms. She kissed him and then reached out to Charlotte to be carried. This was a tender moment. Gillies' parents appeared at the farmhouse doorway. They stood there waiting to greet the newlyweds. Food was being prepared as Gillies eagerly wanted to show Charlotte her new home. Little Charlotte was held by her mother, so that the newlyweds could be alone for a while.

"Close your eyes." Gillies insisted, as he led Charlotte towards the barn.

He picked her up in his arms and carried her through the doorway. Charlotte giggled.

"You can open your eyes now." He said, as he held her still in his arms.

He walked her around the barn. Her gasps of joy at what she saw were endless. Gillies felt good. This meant his months of preparation had gained approval. He carried her to the bed and gently placed her down. He stood there for a moment looking down at her beautiful body. She stretched out her arms, and he went down on her. They laughed with joy that at last they were together in their love nest. They lay there for a while before remembering that there was a meal waiting for them in the farmhouse. They sat around the table all trying to talk at the same time through excitement. Gillies caught the odd wink and smile from his knowing father. Charlotte was so excited about her new home. Gillies sat there admiring the way she was adapting to the naked lifestyle, so full of confidence. They started to agree on the ways in which they could work and live together, yet give privacy to each other. Little Charlotte was beginning to understand that the farmhouse was her home, and the barn was for her brother and his new wife to live. Gillies' father was a master of explaining things.

It seemed strange walking the short distance between farmhouse to barn at the end of the evening. Charlotte flung herself down onto the bed. She looked radiant and happy. Gillies lay down at her side and caressed her. Love was in the air, as this was their first time in sharing the comforts of a bed together. They made love until the early hours of the morning. Sleep came eventually, as did the morning sunlight. Gillies was the first to awake. He eased himself from Charlotte's arms that were around his body. Once outside the barn, he stood for a moment looking across the mountains and valleys. He felt alive and free as he had never felt before. He ran a short distance and then stopped, viewing his world. With outstretched arms above his head, he let his early morning pee flow freely. All was well in his world.

That summer they worked together on the land. Gillies was relieved in seeing how Charlotte had taken to the lifestyle so naturally. He had taught her to milk the goats and to make cheese. They laughed as she plucked her first chicken. This life was far removed from the life she had been brought up in. It had taken a while to dam the waters of the stream that ran through their land. Now they were able to bathe themselves instead of pumping water from the well to fill the tin bathtub. Gillies planned to dam the waters that flowed freely from the higher mountainside. He sketched out his ideas as Charlotte leaned over his broad shoulders watching in pride.

"See. If we build rocks around here in this way," he said, pointing at his sketch, "they will make a large pool to swim in."

It took two months of hard labour to collect the rocks on the cart and move them into position. Dobbin worked hard pulling this daily load up the rough track. He was getting older now, and Gillies was already thinking ahead. His father had listened to his plans, as he smoked his clay pipe sitting in his rocking chair by the fireside. He was proud of his son, the way he had learned to use his head in planning for the future. At times, he had doubted himself about not giving Gillies the chance to go to school to learn to read and write well. But now he was sure that the way they had chosen to live, away from society and fend for themselves, had proved to be right. Gillies had learned from his mother to read and write, and nature had filled his head with knowledge of life. To fish and hunt for food, to toil the land to grow their own vegetables, was all that had been necessary. The facts of life, Gillies had learned from living with the wild animals, watching the stags in mating season, these things had been his education. So now he was listening to his son and his vision for the future. Sadly, he was getting too old himself to do some of the heavy work involved. Little Charlotte was growing fast now, and he had to decide what was best for her now. The past was the past. She was a girl, and things were different for girls in the world. Maybe she should attend school. Many an evening he had talked this over with his wife. Times had changed. Maybe it was the best for their daughter to learn with others. Fate seemed to act in making this choice, for it was one sunny day in July, as they were resting in the fields eating their mid-day meal, when life was about to change for them all. Gillies was the first to catch sight of the dust cloud that appeared way down in the valley below them. This was the sign of wheels on the dusty tracks. He stood up and pulled himself up into a tree for a better view.

"Father, we have visitors."

This was a rare event. For nobody knew of their existence. Soon small horse drawn carriage approached the more level tracks that lead to the farmhouse. Gillies and his father approached the two visitors with caution.

"Good afternoon." One visitor said, announcing himself with outstretched hand.

Gillies and father shook hands. They waited for reason of the visitation. The first man announced that he was from the education department of the near village.

"What is the reason for your visit?" Gillies asked.

"You registered your name in the registry of the church and town records." The second man replied. "We understand that you have a family, one of which is of school age."

Thoughts of past years flashed through the mind of Gillies father. Officialdom had so frustrated him when he married. That is why he had escaped into the mountains. Was this now once again catching up with him?

"That's correct. We choose to educate our daughter in the same way as we did our son."

The two officials stared at Gillies for a moment. It was if they were trying to find words to dispute the fact that he was a fine young man. The first official shuffled his feet before trying to find the way forward in this situation.

"Can you read and write?" Came the question.

Gillies moved forward to the man. He suddenly snatched the papers from the man's hand, glanced down at them and started reading the document aloud. The man remained silent and quite powerless at this stage. Gillies gruffly returned the papers back, smiled, and waited for the next move to be made. His father touched his arm as if to calm the enraged Gillies.

"We have come about your daughter, Charlotte here. We have no issue about your son."

Little Charlotte hung onto her mother's hand. There was a strange silence.

"Can we come inside and discuss this matter?"

"There is no matter to discuss," Eric said. "I would ask you to leave us in peace now."

With that, Eric ushered his wife and Charlotte into the farmhouse. Gillies stood there, naked and with arms folded almost defying the two officials to try to make further efforts to appeal. The two moved towards their carriage.

"We will be back." One of them called out, as they climbed into their seats.

Gillies stood there, his face was stern and showed no fear for the threat. As the carriage turned in a circle to head for the track, one of the men eyed Gillies up and down. Gillies smiled as he heard the words shouted at him.

"Get some bloody clothes on, you perverted lot."

Gillies made no move. He just stood there and waved them goodbye. It had been a brief and heated meeting, but he knew this was not the end of the matter. Charlotte, who had been watching her man's handling of affairs, returned to his side and put her arm around him proudly. That evening, there was an air of unease as they discussed the day's events.

TWELVE

Gillies and Charlotte worked hard daily on their own hectares of land. Gillies stood there, watching his lover as she picked strawberries by the basket load. He felt good in the way she had adapted herself to the lifestyle. Her beautiful body had now become tanned a golden brown. How healthy she looked having lost that pale townspeople look. At the same time, he was being observed by his parents that daily worked their own plot of grounds. How proud they were of their son and his wife. Although they were happy with their lives right now, still the visitation they had had by the authorities hung over their heads. They knew that now the authorities had traces of them through the marriage in the church, and the records housing their names and whereabouts, they were going to have difficult times ahead. For many happy years, they had removed themselves from society. They had fended for themselves, asked for nothing from society, yet here they were, about to be forced to conform with a lifestyle that they had found incompatible to their beliefs. Life was about communing with nature. Nature had most of the answers about life. If one was to listen and learn from nature, life was tranquil and healthy. Gillies was a prime example of their views of life, and how through nature, Gillies had learned much about life the natural way.

Each day, when out in their crop laden land, they thanked their God for their peaceful life. They now asked that same God to protect them from those that might intrude and try and claim their land they owned. As in their early days of living in the wilds of the mountains, this was free land which one could settle on, and could claim rightfully after settlement of three years. This had been done by a mere shake of the hand.

Little Charlotte was immune to all the worries that the others in the family shouldered now. She, like Gillies had, was learning about life through having the questions of life answered but watching and learning from her parents, her brother and his wife, and the animals on their farm. Unlike Gillies, she was not a boy, and so her father did not take her into the wilds of the mountains to hunt for meat and fish for food. She did however help her mother prepare the food for the table. She also was used to seeing the animals caught in the set traps, or shot by skilled arrows, hanging to drain the blood from their bodies. But by spending more time with her mother, she learned from the books and stories told her, as they waited at home in the farmhouse for the return of Gillies and her gather from hunting all day. She also was learning from Charlotte. They had both become very close now, and her sister-in-law would spend endless hours teaching her leanings from having been to school. Little Charlotte was growing into becoming a learned young lady in her own right. It was a hot summer's day in July, when Little Charlotte had seen the dust rise from the track, and the sight of visitors, four of them, arriving by horse drawn cart. She called out to her mother, and they both stood there in the farmhouse doorway, fearing the worst. One of the men touched his hat, as he stepped down from the carriage. He had been one of the two men that had called that fatal day. He introduced himself in an official way, and handed Marian a document. The others in the carriage sat watching. The man held out his hand again as if to ask for the document back, so as to read it aloud to her. There was a silence between them as Marian unrolled the document and started to read it. Her legs were unsteady now. She sat on the stool by the doorway. Little Charlotte pulled a face at the man. She hated him for being there.

Marian reached out her hand to Little Charlotte to take hold of. The document was the one that she had feared would arrive one day. It was a court order for Little Charlotte to attend school. Dates were heavily underlined in the document for attendance at school. Charlotte, who had been working in the cottage gardens, hurried towards the

gathering. All four visitors watched her in her nakedness. This was the young woman that they had known from the town. There were no signs of acknowledgement either way. Charlotte reached out and read the document. She comforted Marian. They were not in shock. It was what they had been expecting this day, so anger was their reaction. The three of them huddled together as the man and his party of officials watched on. The man cleared his throat to speak.

"I have to advise you that the document you have been summoned with is bound by law. The date is clearly written in the document, and your daughter must be in attendance. Failure to abide by the court ruling will result in further action, and heavy fines imposed. You would be unwise to ignore the details of the document."

Oh, how Marian wished Eric was at her side now. She went to speak, but her voice would now allow words to pass her lips. Little Charlotte stamped her bare foot on the ground. The man looked at her actions, yet said nothing. He turned, and climbed back onto the carriage. Once again, he touched his hat, and the horse drew the carriage back down the track, and then they were gone. Charlotte turned and comforted the tearful Marian. Little Charlotte went into the farmhouse and played with her toys. She was feeling insecure now, and this was her way of shutting out the world from her mind. As for Marian, she knew that this could well be the end of their freedom. The evening was drawing in now. Marian sat there, searching for sight of Eric and Gillies. Charlotte had prepared food, but Marian was not hungry. Charlotte sat there with her, but comfort from her was not what was needed, Marian just wanted her man to come home. It was nearly dark now as the two men in her life appeared, carrying a wild boar with its legs tied together and a sturdy branch from a tree supporting the weight of the beast. Their joy of the days hunting was soon dampened, as they listened to the troubles of Marian's day. Eric sat by the fire in his rocking chair. He dragged smoke from his clay pipe, and puffed heavy clouds of smoke into the air. The mood of the farmhouse was low. Few words were spoken as they all sat there within their own thoughts. Gillies managed to hang the wild boar up with a rope strung over the beams in the outhouse. Usually this was done with laughter and pride of their days hunting, but now it was more of a duty. That night in bed he would have had made love to Charlotte to relieve the tensions of hunting from his body. Charlotte would ride her lover, and there would be joyous laugher as she pleased her man. Tonight though, they lay there in each other's arms deep in thought for the future. Next morning, the usually high-spirited gathering for breakfast was lacking. Truly the visitation of officials had brought darkness to their lives. This mood carried through until the day

approached for Little Charlotte to attend school. Gillies and Charlotte had ridden into town the week before. At first Little Charlotte had refused to get dressed, did not want to eat her breakfast, and when she was taken to the cart, where Dobbin was waiting to take them to town, she refused to climb up into the seat.

Eventually when she had calmed down, they had driven to town to meet the head of school. Charlotte was familiar with the routine of school, but received a cold reception. She was seen as the young woman with no shame by living wild in the mountains. She was beginning to realise that the image that people had of their free lifestyle lacked understanding. She had thought often of the day the officials arrived at the farmhouse. Why four of them?

It was clear now in her mind that the town's people lived very shallow lives, and the thought of seeing a naked woman was a sexual thrill to the men, and a damming look of disapproval from the minds of women. So as she and Gillies sat there in the office of the head of school, they felt they had the advantage over her. Their lives were much broader than the townsfolk. Little Charlotte had been made to feel nervous as she sat there listening to her future. They were shown around the small school. Little Charlotte was shown where she would be sitting. She looked around at the children's paintings hanging on the walls. Her own paintings back home were as good as these. She thumbed through some of the reading books on the tables. Some of these she had read already. Why did she have to attend school? She waited her turn to speak, but the head of school was not really letting her do so. There was a cold feeling towards her, which was obvious. Little Charlotte's family did not want her to have to attend school, and the school head was not keen to have her there. As they returned home on the cart, all three talked these matters over. Little Charlotte was nervous now. Gillies comforted her. Once home again, Little Charlotte ran to her mother, not with excitement of the day's events, but more of nervous sorrow. Her mother consoled her, but this was of little comfort to her. That evening they talked about the day's events and how it was going to be possible for them to get Little Charlotte to school daily as the journey took over two hours. Dobbin was not getting any younger either.

Sleepless nights were had by all as the school day drew nearer. Eric had talked of having to move from the farmhouse and finding a house or rooms in the town. The thought of having to change their lifestyle to conform to the outside society that they had abandoned years ago, was frightening. He would have to find work, but what could he do? He had no skills other than farming the land. So the day arrived. Little Charlotte cried and screamed as she was carried by her father to the cart. Marian comforted her as they set off. Gillies and Charlotte watched on helplessly. The day had started with a black cloud hanging over it. They worked in the cottage garden, having milked the goats and fed the livestock. The day seemed long as they toiled away almost in silence. Their thoughts were with Little Charlotte. Marian had nervously approached the school on arrival in the town. She had felt that all eyes were on her, as she struggled with Little Charlotte through the school gates and into the school building. Here she was greeted by the class teacher. The greeting was polite, yet cold. Little Charlotte was dragged away. Marian felt as if she wanted to take her away from this dreadful scene and run back into the safety of the mountains where they belonged. Why couldn't these people and their rules leave them alone to live their lives in peace? Marian brushed her hands down her frock for they were wet with fear. This was all too much for her to deal with, let alone her little daughter. Eric was waiting for her. He helped her up into the cart, and they sat there lost in a world so strange to them. With Dobbin tethered to a rail outside the general store, the two of them wandered around feeling quite lost. Their heads buzzed with the business of what was going on around them. It was as if they were walking in a mist with eyes not in focus. It was a strange feeling.

Eric browsed over notices that appeared in the store window on a

board. **Rooms to let.** He then looked at notices for workers

wanted. He found only a few. Wages were not enough to pay for

even the smallest of rooms for a family of three. What were they to

do.? They sat up on their cart. It was as if their whole world had

come to an end. There was no way they could possibly take and

fetch Little Charlotte daily. Dobbin was not getting younger either.

They sat there for what seemed ages trying to find ways around

their problem. Marian cried a little on Eric's shoulder for comfort.

Why had their peaceful life suddenly come to an end?

The sun was now high in the sky, which told them that it was mid-

day. Workers were coming out of their work places for lunch.

They watched the scene as men sat down on the sidewalks

smoking and drinking together. Their faces seemed sad. Was this

the life that Eric was to have to join? Suddenly they heard a

friendly voice call out.

"Hello, how are you both?"

Eric looked down to see Daniel, the best man from the wedding.

"What are you doing here in town? Nice to see you again."

"Thank you. We have had to bring Little Charlotte to school."

"That's a long way to travel."

Eric got down from the cart and shook Daniel by the hand. Marian gave him a wave.

Daniel listened to Eric's plight. His face showed genuine concern.

There was silence for while as Daniel digested their problem. The first time he had met Gillies' parents, he had been in awe of their lifestyle. Now he could see that, due to the fact that society had rules to conform to, there seemed no justice for those that chose to live peacefully outside these rules. He too disliked the way he had to conform to his elders in the town. As he paced up and down on the road, he patted Dobbin who had been tethered there for hours. Suddenly he quickened his stride and returned to cart.

"Look, I have an idea. Charlotte's parents have rooms spare in their house. They also could do with some extra money." Daniel said, scratching his head as he spoke.

"What are you telling me?" said Eric.

"Well why don't you consider asking them if they can help for the time being. You can't do this daily trek to school. I'm sure they would help."

"No, I couldn't." Eric replied.

"Would you like me to speak to them for you?"

"It's very nice of you to bother, but really, we will manage."

They shook hands again. Daniel smiled up at Marian.

Eric climbed back onto the cart. Marian looked deep into his worried eyes, but she knew her husband well. He was too proud a man to ask such a thing. Worried as they were, they walked to length of the small high street several times waiting for school to finish. Too tired for words, Marian had fallen asleep on Eric's shoulder. It was the sound of children's laugher that made Marian lurch awake suddenly. She watched as the playground emptied of children slowly. There were one or two stragglers making their way out towards the pathway when Little Charlotte appeared.

Marian called out to her. Little Charlotte started running towards her parents. There were tears in her eyes as she slumped down on the cart seat. Marian cuddled her and used her thumb to wipe a tear away.

"What on earth is the matter?"

"Leave her be woman. Let's make our way home." Eric said.

Dobbin was pleased to be on the move again. It was as if he knew the situation as well. During the two hour journey, Little Charlotte spoke about her day in just short bursts between bouts of sobbing. It was when in sight of the farmhouse her sobbing turned to smiles. Gillies had been waiting for their return. Little Charlotte jumped off the cart before it reached the courtyard. She ran towards Gillies outstretched arms. They were a family again that evening. Little Charlotte began to laugh again as she told eagerly events of the day. She had been told to read to the class from a book she had never read before. All eyes had been on her as she read almost without fault. In the afternoon's art class, her painting was chosen to hang on the wall with several of the others, but the teacher had no words of praise. This had made her unhappy. Charlotte, who had been listening, smiled. She knew the teacher in question. Little Charlotte had done well. The truth of the situation was due to the tales of where and how Little Charlotte lived. They were curious and cruel. Kids were like that. Eric talked about his meeting up with Daniel. Charlotte listened without comment. Little Charlotte played with her toys a while before being put to bed. She could not understand why she had to go to bed earlier than usual. Gillies lay with Charlotte in their bed that night discussing the problem. Charlotte firmly insisted that they should both take turns in taking the school run. The early morning sun filtered through their bedroom window. Gillies was feeling amorous. His advances to Charlotte were rejected jokingly. She teased him about his arousal as he tried to trap her onto the mattress. Oh, how she wanted him, but this was an important day. Gillies sat there naked at the foot of their bed watching Charlotte washing herself down in front of him. Her hands ran soap over her breasts in a seductive way. She giggled at his frustrations. Oh, how she wanted him. In total retaliation, his got off the bed, and without trying to hide his erection, he walked past her, and stood a few yards away from the barn and stood proudly peeing with his erection still firm. Charlotte stood in the barn doorway and watched the comical scene. He stood there, hands behind his head, smiling back at her. They were both still in good humour when steering Dobbin in the direction of the town. Little Charlotte found their mood made her laugh and partly forget about school. All three held hands as they walked Little Charlotte through the gates of the school. They waved to her, promising that they would be waiting for her at the

end of school time. Gillies untied Dobbins reins from the rail.
Dobbin snorted as if he had memories of yesterday's long wait in
the heat of the sun. Charlotte was excited that she was able to pay
her parents a visit. Gillies pulled on the reins and headed the cart in
the direction of his in-laws house. With Dobbin tethered and
watered in the shade of a tree, they made their way towards the
house. There were shouts of joy as they greeted each other.

"Well look at you." Her mother said, holding Charlotte at arm's
length. "Don't you look healthy? Is this really my daughter?" She
laughed.

Gillies smiled with pride as he watched the scene. He shook hands
with Francis, but found this turned into an embrace. This indeed
was a welcoming that he had not quite expected. For at the back of
his mind, he had always had that feeling that he had taken
Charlotte from them and introduced her into a lifestyle they were
not best pleased with. He felt good now, as his fears were
unfounded. A pot of tea was made, and cakes were handed around
as they sat chatting excitedly. Gillies watched Charlotte as the
conversation edged towards the situation of his own parents. Her
parents listened and tutted as she explained what had been

happening. The conversation moved from this problem briefly. There was laughter as they talked over past months. Francis, although listening, was deep in his thoughts. The conversation returned to the plight of Gillies' parents. It was quite a problem. Francis ushered his wife out into the kitchen in the pretence of preparing food for lunch time. She laughed at his actions by asking him what had come over him, as he never ever helped her usually.

Gillies heard snippets of conversation that drifted through from the kitchen. He looked at Charlotte as her face was starting to show hints of smiles as she listened too.

As they sat eating their meal of meat and salad, with pieces of bread torn from the large loaf that had been freshly baked, Francis cleared his throat to speak.

"Gillies. How do you think your parents would feel if we suggested that we would like to help by offering them rooms here in our home?"

Gillies sat there for a moment as if surprised at the suggestion. He glanced across the table at Charlotte. Her face at first looked puzzled, and then she teased a smile. He knew all along that when she had suggested taking turns in taking Little Charlotte to and from school, she had pre-planned this discussion with her parents.

"It's a very generous offer. I am not sure that they would be too happy with giving up their lifestyle and having to live in a town again. There is also a question of what my father would do for work."

"Well the offer is there. Your father could help me with my work as a carpenter. I could do with help, as new buildings are planned for developing the west side of town."

Gillies felt Charlotte's foot reach out under the table and nudge his leg.

"Well thank you. You are very kind. I will tell my father. It is their turn to bring Little Charlotte to school tomorrow. Maybe he could visit you to talk about your kind offer."

Once outside the house and climbing up onto the cart, Gillies smacked Charlotte on her rear. She laughed and pushed him back, his foot slipping from the step. This playfulness was watched by her parents as they stood waving goodbye. They were now sure that their daughter was happy in her new way of life. Little Charlotte was waiting at the school gate for them. She waved a sheet of paper in her hand looking excited this time. Gillies helped her up onto the cart, she giggled as she showed them her sheet of paper. It was only her second day at school and she had won a gold star for her writing. The journey back home was happier this time. Gillies just knew that his mother's teaching had proved to be as good as any schools. As soon as they arrived at the farmhouse, Little Charlotte ran excitedly into her mother's arms. Gillies watched this scene, and the way his sister, having handed her mother the sheet of paper from school, then ran indoors to remove all her clothes. Gillies, although he knew that moving into town was the solution to the problem, knew how his parents and his sister were going to miss living naked and free with nature. How would he and Charlotte manage without them on the farm? That evening, both he and Charlotte explained the offer that had been made to help solve the problem. Little Charlotte listened intently.

"I don't want to live in the town. I hate it there. I want to stay here. Please don't let it happen." She cried out. "I'll run away. I hate clothes. I hate wearing shoes." She sobbed.

Eric had to make a decision. Their lives would never be the same again. All of their lives they had fought for their freedom, and now that was being taken from them. He sat there in his rocking chair for most of the night with his mind in a spin. Marian tried to persuade him to take some sleep in bed, but his mind was troubled. That night, none of the family slept. It was as if their world had ended. Even Dobbin in the morning seemed troubled. He shook his head as Eric tried to strap his reins and bridle. Gillies and Charlotte watched and sadly waved as they watched the cart disappear into the distance. This was a sad day they were facing.

THIRTEEN

A month passed, and somehow life on the farm began to return to normal. Gillies family had reluctantly moved out of the farmhouse and were trying to settle their lives in town. Little Charlotte was assured that during school holidays the family would be together at the farm. Eric had found the work easier, compared with working the farm. The two wives found that they were company for each other in the house. Gillies and Charlotte were finding that their own lives as newlyweds more free to make love together. There was something exciting in making love in the hay, with the sun on their backs. They had to rethink their lives now. The produce from the farm was far more than they required for their own table. Even the goat's milk and cheese was so plentiful that they decided that it was time to sell at the market. This meant that twice a week Dobbin was harnessed, and Gillies set off for the nearest village to the west of the region. His stall was set up in the square, and soon their produce was popular with the villagers. Within a month of visits to the village, people were asking where his farm was.

Friendships were beginning to form between the small gathering of stall holder's and Gillies. He was challenged one morning about his nude lifestyle. As he sat with his new friends, they listened keenly. Some smiled; some wore frowns on their faces. To Gillies, this was so natural a way of life he had been born into, but to try and explain it to people this way was difficult. A week later, and after a few joking remarks he heard drifting across from the stallholders, he threw down the challenge.

"Listen." He said. "I would invite you to visit us up there in the mountains next weekend, as long as you don't expect us to dress like this." He said, tugging at his shirt. There was laughter, yet the challenge raised curiosity amongst some. The talk of this invite spread beyond the stall holders. The word spread to the village folk that bought his produce. It was the young couple who, as they selected some of the vegetables with care, they asked if Gillies was a 'naturist'.

"Naturist. What's a naturist?" he asked the couple.

They had been taking a holiday in Germany when they stumbled across a naturist reserve. The young man explained the experience. Gillies listened with interest. The young man went on to tell Gillies that, since that holiday, they had learned that there were several such groups of people that preferred to live naturally with nature. From this conversation, the couple were invited to visit the farm that weekend. That evening, on his return to the farm with Dobbin, he excitedly relayed to Charlotte what he had found out. In a way, they both found relief in the knowledge that they were not alone in the desire of wanting to live as they did. They laughed at the title they had inherited.

They excitedly began to plan as to how to conduct the weekend ahead.

"We could roast a pig." Charlotte said. 'We could have the two tables from the farmhouse out here with stools. Lemonade and wine would be nice to offer everyone."

"We would have to bake lots of bread." Gillies suggested. "I think we should receive them as we live. It will be up to all that attend to decide if they want to be a naturist."

They laughed at their new title. Wasn't it strange that they had lived like, and not knowing that out there in the bigger world, others were living as they were? The next few day's saw them hectically preparing for the big day in their lives. Gillies had to select the pig to roast. When he hunted for wild boar, it seemed natural to kill and then roast the beast, but this was one of his own pigs. The killing only took a quick slit of the pig's throat. It was instant and painless, but never the less, emotional. The morning of the open day at the farm arrived. Gillies was awake early, almost before the sunrise. The fire that had been kept alive was rekindled. As arranged, Charlotte was to help lift the pig onto the spit and hoisted over the burning embers. Bread was baked in the farmhouse oven. The smell of freshly baked bread made them both feel happy, and ready for the day ahead. With tables laid out under the grapevine for protection from the hot sunshine, they awaited their new friends. The sun was high in the sky, which told Gillies that the first visitors would arrive soon. It was at this stage that they realised just what they were taking on. Would these people just be coming for the fun of being in the company of naked people, or had they a genuine love of nature that they wanted to share with other like-minded folk. Too late to worry now. Gillies caught sight of dust rising from the dusty tracks that led up to the farmhouse. He hurriedly rotated the pig again on the spit. Charlotte brought out the red wine, bread and goat's cheese and placed them on the wooden tables that had been scrubbed white. She stood there looking at their efforts. She smiled as Gillies walked over and placed his arm around her naked waist. She looked radiant. Oh, how he loved her and their life together. Two horse and carts arrived together. Gillies welcomed them as they stepped down from the carts and looked around to see the beauty of the farm. There was no eyeing of their nudity. They all introduced themselves with handshakes and air kisses on cheeks. There was no sign of being awkward from the first four of their guests.

"Can we change out of our clothes here, or would you prefer us to do that in the farmhouse?" David asked. He was the young man that had first informed Gillies of his venture in Germany. Charlotte just raised her hands, smiled, then left David to decide. Once he had started to remove his clothes, the others followed by doing the same. It all seemed to be so natural. Jennie, David's wife, had to be helped out of her dress. This caused some laughter between them all. Jake and his wife Joanna were the first to become naked. Jake laughed at his own nakedness, as he strolled around the yard.

"Oh, how I have longed for a day like this day." He called out. "What a beautiful place you have here," he said, "thank you for inviting us."

Soon the wine flowed. They sat there naturally and at ease together. Gillies asked if one of them would help him with the roasted pig. David offered. The sight of yet another carriage arriving started to make this a real party now. As Gillies started to carve the roasted pig, plates were being handed around. The new arrivals joined them and introductions were made again. The new arrivals were Joseph and Emma. Now the scene was set for a wonderful party. Gillies was often the centre of the attraction as they were all curious as to how he had survived living the lifestyle. He was a good story teller. His guests listened to his tales of hunting in the wilds of the mountains.

Laugher turned to singing when Jake, who had arrived with his guitar, began to play. Although Gillies was joining in the singing, he watched the happy scene. It was so nice, peaceful and relaxed. How wonderful it was to see a small group of people, who hardly knew each other, relaxing naked as the day they were born like this. With the music from Jakes guitar drifting off into the background, the conversation became more serious. Gillies was interested in learning more about the naturist reserves that David had visited in Germany. The longer David talked about his experiences, the more Gillies became interested. They both left the party for a stroll around the farm. David remarked that he had never felt so comfortable in nude company. He and Jennie led their lives like this at home, but it was restricting for them. He looked back at the farmhouse at the others sitting there. Gillies stood there with him. His thoughts were as David's. If only life could be like this for like-minded folk.

"You have a many hectares here. How will you manage all this on your own?"

"I am finding it difficult now, to tell you the truth," Gillies replied. "I was thinking about what you were telling us about your holiday in Germany. I have been isolated from the outside world. We are far from lonely, but you all coming today has started to make me think."

They both sat down in the grass. David just had that feeling as to what Gillies was thinking.

"David. Do you think our farm, and all the land we have, would be a good place to open up to these people you talk of called *naturists?* I like that word."

David smiled. He had learned that there were naturist's in Europe some years back, but had only found it on his holiday. He and Jennie had taken to the lifestyle on holiday. Now they were home again, they missed the communal side of the lifestyle.

"Gillies. You have no idea what a great adventure this would be for you and Charlotte. I know we have only met in the past few weeks, but I would love to help you with your dream if you were going to do this."

Gillies suddenly stood up. He beckoned David to follow him. They walked for what seemed ages. David had to run at times to keep up with Gillies in his excitement.

"Look at that level land there. That would make for good a camping area. And look over there," he said excitedly, pointing to the clear water that cascaded down from the mountains, "I could dam that off and make a pool for swimming just there."

David had never seen such a natural landscape carved out by nature. He stood there for a while surveying all before him. His ideas filled his head. He could live the dream as well. They stood there listening to the sound of the water flowing down from above. Excitedly they shared the same vision. Their faces were alive with the dream.

"You, I mean we," David laughed, "we could build the first dam, and then let the water just find its own level and continue to flow down to the next level until it reached the river below. Come, let's climb down to the river and take a look."

They made their way down the steep slopes of the mountainside. They realised that there was a lot to be done by clearing some of the undergrowth. Boughs were held back for each other as they made their way down. Gillies felt good about having a friend like David to share his new dream. He couldn't wait to tell Charlotte of what they had in mind for the future. The farm was going to become a Naturist Reserve. Was this nature sending him a message through David? The sound of the rushing waters from above soon drifted out of earshot. Now there was that silence and calm all around them as the gentle soft sound of stream of pure clear water trickled and weaved its way through the rocks and boulders down into the river. The two young men stood there in amazement at the scene before them. There to their right was a small natural pool. This was a miniature version of the pool they intended to build up nearer the farmhouse. It was as if their thoughts were as one, as they both jumped from the rocks into the pure water of the natural pool. They shouted and laughed as they enjoyed their naked freedom together. The pool was deep enough to swim in, yet shallow enough to be able to stand up in, with the level of water coming up to their shoulders. They both stood there for a moment looking up towards the top of the cliff edge where the cascade of water descended from. It was a beautiful moment as their dream was about to unfold. Suddenly they heard echoes of their names being called out by their friends. Gillies called out aloud, using his cupped hands to help project his answer to them. Soon they could see the others clambering down to join them. Charlotte was the first to appear through the undergrowth.

"We all thought you had got lost. What on earth have you been doing?" She asked.

Soon the group of friends were in the water together laughing and splashing each other. They sat there knowing this was a special new beginning to the future for all of them. Neither Gillies nor

David had mentioned what they had been discussing earlier, but somehow they knew that something very special was happening in their lives. They had listened to Gillies and Charlotte as they had explained their way of life earlier. Now though, they knew their own lives needed to broaden. What was happening to them now was to be the beginning to a new way of life. Once back at the farmhouse, they sat around listening to Gillies' plans. Charlotte sat at his side holding his hand in hers as he spoke of how he intended to dam the waters from the mountain, and make a pool larger than the one they had been swimming in together. He felt Charlotte's hand squeeze his with approval. There were many questions raised, but never a doubtful one. Gillies knew he was sitting with true friends. Friends that wanted to share their lives with nature. They had been living their lives so far, as couples in isolation. Now they had ventured to join with others this naked freedom, the future was exciting. The sun was dipping fast behind the mountain range. Clothes were soon worn again as they began to fill the chill of the evening. The horses were harnessed. It had been good watching their trusted shires together feeding from the green pastures. Gillies smiled and remarked that this had saved him the job of having to cut the meadow. Sadly, the day came to an end. Gillies and Charlotte waved to their new-found friends as their carts disappeared down the track and out of view. They both sat there, way past midnight, talking excitedly about the future. They were about to open up their way of life, and have others join them in the freedom. They were about to open their farm to naturists near and far. There was a lot of work to be done before this could take place, but they knew that their new friends were supportive. Charlotte was worried as to how to go about letting like-minded folk know where they were. Gillies assured her that David had promised to deal with all these details. Between them there was plenty to do. It was to be hard work, but an exciting change to their lives. For the next few days, apart from working in their vegetable gardens, they both took time off to wander around their hectares. They sketched out their ideas as to where tents could be pitched, latrines could be built, and washing facilities placed. One thing they were insistent on was, they wanted their naturist reserve to be in keeping with nature, simple, basic, and a reserve where people could escape for a while from the restrictions of the world out there. A natural peaceful commune, in tune with nature. By the time the weekend came around again, when their friends were due

to join them, they had drawn up a rough plan of the layout of the

reserve. Tables were laid out again under the shade of the grape

vines. Soon their friends could be seen arriving all together. The

dust from the track, as their carts raced in convoy, made clouds of

dust rise into the air. They all greeted each other with excitement.

There was a rather special bond being created between them now.

Wine flowed, and they sat there on the stools and benches, naked

and free again, after a week of working in the textile world.

Chicken salad was the meal. Fruit was brought by Jake from his

stall. They talked excitedly about their own week. It was obvious

that Gillies and Charlotte had had the best week out of all of them.

David joked about his own stall in the market and how he had

wanted to remove his clothes as the sun had shone down on them

all week. Once the meal was finished, Gillies produced his plans

showing their ideas of the layout. They huddled together trying to

estimate how many tent pitches they could spread out across the

area designated for campers. Gillies was insistent that they should

allow individual pitches to be in private and located in quite

remote areas in the mountainside. David laughed and called him a romantic. Gillies however remembered his own small camp in the wilds and the fox that befriended him there. This was the freedom he wanted others to enjoy. It was agreed that the first thing to be tackled was the damming of the waters cascading down from the mountains so as to make the swimming pool safe and secure for young and old to swim in. David was appointed to promote their venture. He had had some experience as he had worked for a while for a local newspaper before starting his own market stall. He had also travelled in Europe for a year. Then of course he had taken a holiday and found out that there were naturist reserves already established. So he was the most experienced out of the group of eight. The next problem to overcome was how many tools they could collectively muster up between them. They assembled around the area where the pool was to be built. Gillies climbed up the rock face where the waters cascaded over. He could visualise from above how great an area the pool would take up. They laughed as he directed each one of them to stand to form a circle and place a rock to mark the area. Once this was done, he joined them again.

"This is where we have to dig down and remove the soil." The pool was going to be quite large. They stood there laughing as Gillies made strides across the area making swimming strokes with each stride. The deep end of the pool would be at the base of the cliff face, and then taper down to a shallow end where the water would then overflow down the mountainside to the next level. Charlotte sketched the idea out on paper, as they sat around the table back at the farmhouse. They had about five months of summer left in which to complete the basic layout of the site. To start with the toilets would be positioned in a central area. Yes, it was going to be quite a basic start, however, Gillies was keen to keep the whole project simple and in keeping with nature. The group listened to his plans, and understood his views. His parents had taken a bold and brave attempt to escape back to nature. Gillies just wanted others to enjoy the same freedom. One thing he insisted on, was to keep the whole project simple and basic. He wanted to see families enjoying nature, to swim naked, to be able to cook food over open fires. He wanted children to enjoy the same things he had. To be free to climb trees, make their own camps, to run through the meadows, to see what nature had to offer over town life. He had a vision, and now he had found friends to share that vision with. David pulled Gillies to one side. He wanted to chat to him in private. They wandered ahead of the others as they all made their way back to the farmhouse. Gillies had a fair idea as to what the conversation was going to be.

"Gillies. Look, Jennie and myself are so excited about the project; we thought it would be an idea to throw our lives completely into this."

"Do you mean you would want to devote more time to this?" Gillies asked.

"Yes, we are prepared to spend what savings we have to help you."

"What about your market stall?"

"I think we could survive about a year without having to make money. But it means asking that big question."

"That being?" Gillies smiled.

"Giving up our little house in the village."

"And?"

"Well I guess you know the answer to that. Could we rent your barn or farmhouse off you? You see, we are both frustrated in living as we are as textiles. When seeing the naturist lifestyle in Germany, well, we knew then what we both wanted from life."

Gillies stopped walking. He stood still for a moment looking down at the ground, as if in deep thought. David stopped at his side not quite knowing if he had gone too far with his thoughts of the future. There was a long silence. Then suddenly Gillies looked up, threw his arms around David in a huge hug.

"So you think it would all work, this crazy idea of mine?"

David returned the hug of emotion. The two stood there embracing the friendship.

"I have no doubts about the venture. God knows, the world needs people like you."

"Well if you have the same beliefs as Charlotte and myself, then yes, the farmhouse is yours to rent. There is one condition though. When my parents and Little Charlotte come to spend the school holidays, you will have to move in with us in the barn."

David kissed him on both cheeks. They shook hands on the deal. That evening in the farmhouse the friends laughed and joked together. The future looked so good for all of them.

Mike Herring

FOURTEEN

David and Jennie moved in and settled down in the farmhouse well. They had at last found their freedom of life. The pool was the first project on the quite massive list of things to be done to make this a natural reserve for naturists. The work of moving rocks and earth to build the natural pool took three weeks. There was one final effort that all eight friends took part in. The pool was functioning as planned. They stood on the level above the pool, watching the water cascading down from above. Gillies wanted slight adjustments to the flow of water. They moved quite heavy rocks to narrow the channel. As they built the walls of the channel, each rock was moved until the flow was correct. They stood there with pride, as they saw the results of their labours. The water was now flowing well, and the slope they had slaved away to create, worked well. At the far end the water flowed over the edge and cascaded down to the next level. They had created the perfect pool. The final test came when they had to jump and dive into the deep end just below them. Gillies elected to be the first to test out their work. With a shout that seemed to echo around the mountainside, Gillies, took a deep breath, held his nose, and leaped into the depths below. His wife and friends waited anxiously as they watched him disappear under the surface, then suddenly appear shouting and laughing the success.

"Wow that was great feeling. I never touched the bottom. It's really perfect and safe. Come you lot, join me." Gillies called out.

His voice had only just echoed up to them when, one by one, they leaped down into the pool with shouts of joy. They sat in the wall of the pool surveying their hard work.

It was idyllic. The sound of the clear water cascading down into the pool sounded like music to Gillies' ears. How lucky he was in having been brought up with nature. Now he was going to be able to share this lifestyle with others. David had worked hard on advertising the reserve. There was much to be done before they could receive likeminded folk into their reserve. Clearings had to be made for tents to be pitched. Water had to be made accessible. Toilets had to be located in each area. All these had to be prepared, as well as continuing to sell vegetables in the market to earn money. The women tended to the vegetable plots, whilst the heavy manual work was for the men to do. It was nearing the end of summer before the plans became visible. The local newspaper ran an article on their venture. David was not too happy that the right message had been written. In the village market place there was a lot of enquiring remarks made. They all sat down one evening to discuss the best way to open the reserve to the public. It was decided to announce an open day. A day where people could come and look around, swim in the pool and enjoy food and drink. They would allow the public to walk around clothed, but leave it up to them if they wanted to enjoy the freedom of naturism. There would be a strict rule that swimming would be nude. The eight of them would continue to be seen naturally naked, just to show their way of life was healthy. The date was agreed as being the first weekend in April. Posters were put up in the village and surrounding areas. Now they had to just wait for the day. They had placed a post box down at the entrance where the track led off the road that ran between village and town. Daily, one of them would check the box. January and February passed without mail being seen. Then David excitedly collected five letters from the post-box in March. That weekend they read the letters again and again.

The general feeling was of curiosity. That was a good reaction to have, David had suggested. With just one month to go before opening day, this was encouraging. They had concentrated all their efforts on getting one large area ready. The grass was cut short, plus it had a wash unit and toilet block built. The water supply had been the hardest project for them to tackle. It was quite basic, but it worked. Rain was not plentiful; however, they had managed to construct a shower. This consisted of four wooden poles with a platform some ten feet high. An old bucket hung there, with holes made in the bottom, which acted as the shower. There was a ladder for a person to climb up to the platform, where they could pour water from a metal bath, that could either catch rain in, or be filled from the hand pump below. The person above then poured water into the bucket below, riddled with holes, for the person below taking a shower. The group of friends took turns in taking a shower from their invention, so basic, but it worked well. And so with this work completed, they awaited the opening day with excitement, plus a few nerves. The word had got around the area. They had chosen a Sunday as the opening day in the hope that this would attract more interest.

It was the Thursday market day prior to the Sunday opening day that the real interest seemed to grow. Gillies and David had agreed to be there on their stall. They had notices posted around just about everywhere possible and leaflets to hand out. People were curious as to what the Sunday would be like, and what would happen. At the end of the day as they were clearing up, it was then that they realised that the interest was truly there. Many would be coming just to be curious. Never the less, the interest was there. Gillies had watched a few groups of youths smirking as they read the posters. Wasn't it sad that they possibly had never been out of their clothes and seen others naked before? They would obviously be the ones that would come to ogle at the scene.

There were those that just made it clear that they thought it weird to live like they did. However, there were a few that showed genuine interest. It was going to be an interesting day. What was going to be exciting was seeing his parents and Little Charlotte again. They had been excited for him, yet unable to help.

Mike Herring

FIFTEEN

Sunday morning saw the whole area around the farmhouse become festive looking. Stalls were laid out with food that had been prepared. The wild boar was on the roast, and there were potatoes ready to bake. Cider had been brewed in stone jars, and jugs of lemonade were standing in the shade of the vines. There was an air of excitement, mixed with a little nervous tension between the eight friends that had worked so hard for this important day. They had no idea how the project would be received. The sun was now high in the sky when the first of the visitors started to appear. Some arrived by cart, while others could be seen walking the long track from the road up to the farmhouse. It was as if they had organised themselves into small groups. Within an hour there were over thirty visitors gathered around the farmhouse. David had been chosen to make the introductions. From an outsider's view of the scene, it could seem as laughable, funny in the contrast between the group of eight naturists and the textile visitors. For a while there was unease until David stepped forward to greet them. He looked around to see if there were others arriving up the track.

"Welcome." David said, looking around the gathering. "May I introduce you to Gillies? This young man has lived here since he was born. He has hunted for food and grown up in the wilds of this mountain range as you see him now."

Gillies stood forward feeling quite confident standing there naked in front of them. There was a slight applause as he waved a welcome to them. David smiled.

"We would invite you to take a look around the reserve. For those of you that would like to experience what it is like swimming naked for the first time, please take a dip in our pool down there. I would ask that all clothing must be removed before you take a swim. The sun is hot, and the water is just nice at this time of day. For those of you that are not sure if you want to be that brave, please feel free to wander around the camping area and return back here for food and drinks, all free. Please just enjoy yourselves on this glorious day."

Gillies could see one or two of the youths from the market. They were the first to wander off down to the pool. His fears of trouble were unfounded. Once down by the pool, they stripped off their clothes, joking and pushing each other in fun. Soon they were in the pool, laughing and calling out to each other. Some had dared to climb up to the first ledge and jump down into the pool. This was just the day Gillies had dreamed of as he watched the scene. Soon others gathered around to watch. It was not long before people were stripping off their clothes to join the youngsters. David had stayed back at the farmhouse to greet new arrivals. He was aware that half of the village had turned out to experience the day. The roasted boar was ready to be carved. Gillies stood there carving away as eager hands thrust their plates forward for a portion. Salad and potatoes added to the piled plates. David estimated that here were a good seventy people all gathered around the farmhouse. Hardly any had bothered to put their clothes back on. The youths mingled with their elders, naked and uninhibited. Charlotte stood at Gillies side. She held his hand and squeezed it. They smiled at each other. This was just unbelievable. People from the village were beginning to ask questions about future visits. David thought this was the time to speak up again. He explained that this was going to be a camp site where all could enjoy the freedom of being natural and free with nature. People from other countries were expected as well.

"You are all welcome to come and visit at weekends, or come and stay for holidays. It will be open to all, as long as you have a respect for others privacy. Clothes can only be worn if the weather is not kind to us. Swimwear must never be worn in the pool."

Offers of help were made, even from the youths. There were only a few that left early, as they were not sure about being nude in company. That evening, it was great seeing the teenagers, about twenty or more, sitting around the camp fire that had been lit down near the pool area. They were comfortable and relaxed sitting around on the grass chatting and laughing with each other without feeling uncomfortable. It was getting quite late. The sun was dipping down below the mountain range. As it was quite warm still, there were little signs of these youngsters wanting to leave. Some of the elderly couples had joined them. It all seemed so natural now. Gillies, who had been wandering around to see that all was well, was approached by a couple of the youths. They stood there in front of him. Their white bodies, in contrast to the dark brown healthy body of Gillies were quite extreme. Their white bodies and their brown arms showed where they had at least rolled up their sleeves.

"Can we come here at weekends, if we helped you around the camp site?

Gillies smiled at the request as he surveyed the young group. He felt good, as this told him that this opening day had been a success. "I think we could arrange that. Not sure where we could sleep you as we haven't more than two tents so far. I'm sure we could work something out."

The youths smiled. Handshakes took place and thanks received. Gillies watched the happy group turn and run back towards the pool. He knew that in time these white limbed youths would turn out to be healthier for the venture. The evening was drawing to a close. Gillies, Charlotte, David and Jennie watched the last of the visitors' departure down the track. They sat in the farmhouse, picking at the remains of the food and taking sips of wine as they discussed the day's events. David had been holding back on some news. He had received a letter from friends they had made on holiday in Germany. Their friends wanted to take a camping holiday with them.

"This is how news will get around. Let's hope that we get more visitors from abroad." He said, waving the letter in the air.

Monday morning seemed a little quiet as David and Gillies walked around the reserve, looking to see if any damage had been caused. To their delight, all seemed well. The visitors had respected the grounds. Yes, there were odd screwed up paper bags dropped here and there. This meant that waste bins would have to be placed around the site in future. They laughed as they found a pair of pants on the ground at the side of the pool. Apart from that, the site had been left in a tidy state. Work on the land continued, as vegetables had to be dug up and prepared for market. Sales of vegetables had gone well on open day. What was a disappointment though, Gillies' parents had not been with them. Gillies was worried. He would have to ride into town and find out if all was well with his family. David and Jennie insisted that they could manage the market so that Gillies could visit town. Dobbin was in for a hard day on market day. Once the vegetables had been unloaded at the stall, Gillies got Dobbin on the trot towards town. It had been ages since visiting the town. Now he felt more secure and confident than those early days when first meeting Charlotte. David had given him leaflets about their naturist camping. He was excited about seeing his family again. Dobbin was tethered near the water trough under the shade of trees. He heaved the sack of vegetables off the cart. The weight of these on his back made him hurriedly reach the steps leading up to the front door of the house. The door was opened by Little Charlotte. Gillies had only just put down one weight, only to have to carry another. Little Charlotte leaped into his arms with joy. He lifted her up and hugged her.

"Goodness me, you are getting a big girl. What have you been eating?" He joked.

Little Charlotte kissed and hugged him, almost taking his breath away. He could see tears in her eyes. These were not all of joy, but of sorrow.

"Hey, why the tears?"

"Because I'm so happy you are here, but Daddy is ill and Mummy is worried."

Gillies kissed her again as he placed her down. He hurried into the house and called out for his mother, as he hurried upstairs. He was greeted at the bedroom door. His mother's face was a mixture of smiles and sadness. She hugged him and kissed him, and then she led him into the bedroom. His father was asleep. Gillies could see a shadow of a father he knew. He sat down on the side of the bed and reached for his father's hand. It felt lifeless to his touch. There was a slight movement as his father moved his head on the pillow. His face looked gaunt. This was not the father he knew. His mother placed a hand on his shoulder in an attempt to comfort him. After a while they left the bedroom. Gillies looked back over his shoulder as he left the room. He felt sad, yet angry that he had not been told about his father's health. Once downstairs, Gillies sat down in the kitchen. Not a word had been exchanged between them. He questioned his mother. He could see tears in her eyes as she wandered around making a pot of tea. She had aged. Little Charlotte was no longer little. How a few months had changed both of them. His father had been working hard when suddenly his chest had begun to pain him. Back in the mountains this man had been so strong and healthy. Now he was a shadow of himself. Gillies listened to his mother as she tried to explain the past months. The three of them had been unhappy living in the town.

"Why did you not get a message through to me?" Gillies asked.

"Why didn't you come and see us?" His mother asked.

They sat there in silence, each deep in thought at their questions. Gillies went out into the front porch and sat down on the steps. As he sipped his mug of tea, he suddenly felt so guilty. Guilty of the way he had been so engrossed in his own life. He then reflected back on how this had come about. They were all so happy living their lives up there in the mountains naked and free sharing life with nature. There life had been so simple and happy. Then along came authority. The system, the one they had never encountered before that cart bringing two officials from the town arrived demanding that Little Charlotte went to school. He placed his now empty mug down on the step, and walked down the street. As he walked, he kicked stones in anger. Why was he angry? Was it about his own selfish ways in wanting to remain in the mountains? Was it about the stupid official rules of society that changed the way the family lived? Had he been so wrapped up in his own life with Charlotte?

Suddenly he heard the sound of footsteps behind him. A hand reached for his. It was Little Charlotte. He stopped, and once more took her into his arms. He knew then, that the family was the most important thing in life. It was society rules, laws, all made up by single minded officials that had made their lives change. As he returned to the house, he had made up his mind. He was going to take the family back with him. Let the law come and try to do the same again. He had become the man he was. His parents had brought him up, educated him, and let nature enter his heart and body. Now he was in a strong position of supporting Charlotte and his family. Once inside the house again, he composed himself. His mother listened as he outlined his views as to how they could get back to the way they were. His plan was to come back within the week and take all three of them back to their natural home in the mountains. His mother cried as she hugged him. This is what she had wished for. The town life was not for her. They had been so unhappy. Yes, she had enough knowledge to educate Little Charlotte. Her fear was how the officials would react to this. Gillies assured her that this was for him to worry about. He went upstairs again to see his father. As he sat on the bed, he held his father's hand again. These were the hands of a man that had worked hard all his life. The hard skin and scars were evidence of this. He knew that his father could hear him as he outlined what he intended to do. He was sure that his father understood him by the hint of a smile that crossed his face. Their hands clasped stronger

as Gillies said his farewells. He leaned down and kissed his
father's cheek.

Neither he, nor his mother, told Little Charlotte of their plan to
return home. They knew that this was best, for fear of her
excitement being known by others. She had never settled at school.
She had from the start been ahead of the others in her class. This
was due to the teaching from her mother. Gillies patted Dobbin as
he climbed up onto the cart and headed home. He looked back as
he headed out of town. He waved back to his mother and sister
who stood cuddling each other. Soon he was on his way home
again, leaving the claustrophobic air of the town behind him. As he
reached the entrance to the rough track that weaved its way up and
down towards the farmhouse, he had the sudden urge to remove his
clothes. Dobbin waited, snorting through his nostrils. He knew he
was home again. Gillies, now in his natural state, slapped the reins,
and the cart wheels made that sound of being home again as they
bumped along the rough track. Charlotte greeted him as he climbed
down from the cart. They kissed and embraced. She smiled as their
naked bodies touched. Gillies was aware that his semi erection was
felt in the embrace. Charlotte pulled away giving him a teasing

slap on his backside. David had been observing this from the farmhouse doorway. As Gillies greeted him, David jokingly held him at a distance. Gillies placed his hand over his pubic area and smiled. That evening they sat around the meal table listening to Gillies' summing up of his family's situation. David and Jennie quite understood about having to move out of the farmhouse. They planned to divide the barn in two. There was enough space for two bedrooms to be made. As for the living area, they would be communal with this in true naturist style. Gillies and Charlotte made their way back to the barn. They showered together and retired to bed to make wild affectionate love. It was as if he had been away for ages. Gillies rode high above her with strong thrusts; her legs were wrapped around his strong firm body, not ever wanting this love act to finish. They knew that one day Gillies would not withdraw from her as he reached his climax. They would be hoping to make child. Charlotte brushed her hand across his chest as they lay there talking about the future. Gillies knew that Charlotte wanted to have a child. They knew that the timing was not quite now. There were so many things to be done to develop the camping areas if they were to attract naturists from afar. They wanted to make clearings for pitching tents, high up in the mountainside, where folk could share nature alone. This was hard manual work for the small group of eight friends. Gillies reminded himself of the youngster's conversation with him on opening day. They would be a great help if they could be allowed to camp there at weekends and holidays. There was so much to be done. He buried his face in Charlotte's breast as to take his mind off the problems of the day.

Charlotte slept, leaving Gillies thinking about his father's health. He had to get his family out of the town and back into the fresh air of the mountains. The following days found them busy once again. The vegetables and fruit were collected ready for the market which they attended twice a week. The money from this was all they had to live on. This made the opening of the campsite all the more important. At the Wednesday's market, Gillies and David found themselves being questioned about the camping. Some questions were asked with humour, and many were of keen interest. People were tired of not having much more in their lives than just working the land.

As for the youths of the village, they had nothing much in their lives other than leaving school, only to find very little in the way of work. These youths were keen to help Gillies, and his friends, prepare the campsite. They asked for no more than food in return for their help. Offers of tools for the land were offered by some of the older folk that had attended the opening day. Even a tractor was offered by one of the farmers. Gillies had only read books with stories and drawings about tractors. He had never seen one. He knew that Dobbin was getting older, so the tractor would be of great help in getting the heavy work done. The farmer promised to drive it up to them, as neither David, nor himself, knew how to drive the iron monster. News emerged that a new road was going to be built to run between the mountains. This was exciting news, as it would make the access to the camp and farmhouse easier for visitors to find them. At this time, the rough tracks made it difficult for easy travel. On their way back from the market, David collected more mail from the post-box. He read them out aloud to Gillies as they jogged along the long dusty track to the farmhouse. They were to have more naturists arriving from Germany. One letter was from a family in Holland. So it was even more important that the road be completed. It would make it easier for visitors to find them. That evening, talking over the future was the topic as usual. Added to this was now the problem of bringing Gillies' family back to the farmhouse. Gillies was insistent that he would fight off all attempts to have Little Charlotte educated by his mother. David had reservations about this. Gillies teased him that he only doubted that this because he knew no different. David had been educated at school, whereas he had been educated by his mother, plus the fact that nature had played a big part in making him worldlier than him. They both laughed at their difference. Next morning, Gillies set off to collect his ailing father. The others had doubts that this was the right thing to do. Gillies insisted that the only thing that would cure his father was by bringing him home to breathe in the mountain air again.

He no longer felt a stranger as he entered the town. He still hated having to wear clothing just to conform with town folk. He tethered Dobbin outside the house this time. He knew that he might have to carry his father down and out of the house. So Dobbin was not going to be standing there too long. His mother greeted him.

She looked pale and tired. What had living in the town done to her?

"Where is Little Charlotte?" He asked.

"At school. We didn't know what day you were coming."

"Have you packed your belongings?"

"Yes, I have. We have very little, as you well know." His mother said.

Gillies dashed upstairs to see his father. As he entered the bedroom, he could hear his father coughing. It was a deep harsh cough, a cough that rasped in the chest. Gillies raised his father's head up and gave him a sip of water. His father opened his eyes, and there was a hint of a smile on his face.

"Hello father. I have come to fetch, you and take you home."

His father tried to speak, but the words never left his dry mouth. He was very ill.

Gillies dashed downstairs again. His mother was sitting down on the steps of the porch. He sat to comfort her. He knew that he had arrived just in time. His parents were at their lowest now. There was so much to be done. Little Charlotte had to be fetched from school. That wasn't going to be easy. He collected bundles of clothes and personal items from inside the front door, and placed them in the cart. He wanted something for his father to rest on. He was not well enough to sit up in the cart. The mattress from the bed upstairs was going to have to be brought down. Little Charlotte would help him. He headed off in the direction of the school at a brisk pace, watched by his mother who could not quite understand what was happening. Gillies, her son, was suddenly the man of the family. She had to place her trust in him that he was doing the right thing. She managed a smile as she watched Gillies striding towards the school. The children were out in the playground when he arrived. He stood by the fence searching for his sister. There she sat, alone and crouched up across the other side of the playground, alone and looking sad. Gillies waved to her, but she was not looking in his direction. He waited for a while trying to attract her attention. Time was against him, so he couldn't wait any longer. He hurriedly approached her as she sat there. On seeing him, Little Charlotte jumped up and ran towards him. He cuddled her to comfort her. She had been crying. He could see that, as her eyes were red.

"Come along. Hold my hand, we are going home." Gillies told her.

The children watched as he marched across the playground towards the gate. One of the teachers dashed across in an attempt to restrain him. Little was she to know that he was Little Charlotte's big brother. Gillies was polite enough to stop and explain his actions. This proved to be difficult. Two other teachers appeared from the school building to assist. There was a struggle as Gillies clutching his sisters hand, dragged her away from the attempts of teachers to restrain him. He knew he had to move fast.

He explained everything to his sister as they hurried towards the house. Her little face lit up with joy. Once indoors, Gillies went upstairs, raised his father out of bed, placed him down on the floor with just a pillow for his head to rest on. He then folded the feather mattress in two, and carried it downstairs and out into the cart. His mother just stood there watching for a moment. Then suddenly, as if she had been given a new life, she hurried upstairs to aid Gillies with his attempts to carry his father to the cart. The struggle down the stairs was not easy. His father was helpless. Once outside again, Gillies, aided by his mother, laid his father out on the mattress. A blanket was placed over him. The journey back to the farmhouse was slower than usual. Gillies was aware that his father could not stand too much jolting around. His mother and sister sat with father, bathing his forehead with a damp cloth, he had a slight fever. David stood in the courtyard of the farm, waiting to help. Dobbin snorted, as the reins pulled him to a halt. Gillies insisted that he carried his father into the farmhouse and place him down on his own bed again. His father managed a slight smile. It was as if he knew he was at last home to rest. His fever made him drift into sleep patterns. Gillies sat there for a while at his bedside, wondering what to do now. Time would   only tell how serious his condition was. David had unloaded the cart and attended to Dobbin. The poor old horse was getting too old for this amount of work now. The tractor that had been promised would take over some of his duties. Charlotte had prepared food for them all. They sat in the farmhouse around the table, almost in silence. Little Charlotte played happily upstairs in her loft style bedroom. She was not sure what was happening to her life now. One thing she was sure about was the fact that she didn't have to go to school in the morning. She had asked Gillies repeatedly, all the way from the town, to arrival at the farmhouse. That night, hardly anyone slept, apart from Little Charlotte. Gillies eased himself out of his bed. He looked down to see that he had not disturbed Charlotte. He walked

out into the starlit night. His mind was now full of problems Where

had those days gone, the days that were so carefree and had been

happy leading the simple life out here, with nature, playing in the

wilds of the mountains. He wandered down to the pool and dived

in cool water. His head started to clear now. He swam around for a

while before sitting on the rocks at the side of the pool. There was

a sudden swirl of cool wind that seemed to come and go, as if a

door had been opened and shut suddenly. He felt suddenly cold

and uneasy sitting there alone. Was nature sending him a message?

Looking up to the skies he saw a single black cloud drifted across

the moonlight, he knew nature was speaking to him. He ran like a

chased hare back to the farmhouse. Yes, there was a lamp alight

there and the front door was open. As he approached he knew his

fears were true. His mother sat there on a stool outside in the yard.

Gillies ran to her side. She was crying, short sobs of sorrow. He

comforted her by putting his arm around her shoulders. She laid

her head against his body, her hands covering her face. Between

burst of tears, she told Gillies how she feared the end was near for

his father. Gillies dashed to his father's side. He had always remembered how strong a man his father was. Now he looked down on a weakened man. He sat there for a while trying to find words of comfort for his father. There were moments where he knew that his father was hearing him. Their hands communicated and confirmed this. Gillies raised his father's head, trying to get him drink a little water. He placed his head back on the pillow, stood there knowing that the end was near. If he went for a doctor, it would take hours to even reach the town. Just for a moment, Gillies found peace in his mind. His father had lived his life with nature. Now nature was calling him to return. Society and the world out there had destroyed him. Why had they enforced him to conform to their life in the town? He had provided for him and the family. Gillies looked around the farmhouse. Every stone and bolder had be collected from the mountainside and laid solidly in place by his own hands. The rafters were solid and firm, the wood selected from the forests around them. His father's love would always remain there with them, like a memorial. He felt tears suddenly blurring his vision. He knew he had to be strong now for his mother and Little Charlotte. Time would spell out the fate of his father. There was little they could do. He returned to his mother's side. She was a little more composed now that he was at her side. They sat together at his father's bedside in silence. The sun entered the farmhouse. Gillies had dozed off to sleep a little as he had sat in his father's chair. Charlotte joined them. She had been aware of their sorrow, but knew that it had best to have left them alone. Now it was time for her to keep her strength. She prepared breakfast. David and Jennie entered the farmhouse to be of comfort. Gillies wandered outside into the yard. Once again he looked up to the skies.

The sky was clear with blue, yet there was one black cloud lingering just over the peak of the mountain range. He stood there watching its slow drift towards the sun. Wasn't nature wise, beautiful, yet cruel at times. He went back indoors, without a mention of what he believed was happening. It was just a matter of comforting his mother and waiting. An hour later, the cloud drifted over the sun. The room darkened. Gillies knew this was the time that his father was to leave them all. He took hold of his mother's hand in his. He then placed their hands with his father's hand. Moments later, he passed away in peace.

SIXTEEN

Gillies, helped by David, Jake and Joseph had dug the grave up in the mountainside, where he, and his father, had spent many happy times camping. They returned back to the farmhouse after a long day's toiling. The world seemed to have stopped for them all. There was sadness as they prepared for the funeral. There had been discussions about rules and regulations of townsfolk over matters such as this. Gillies was firm on what he was doing. He was returning his father to nature. They encouraged Dobbin to haul the ageing cart up the steep slopes and uneven ground. The hurriedly prepared wooden coffin was placed in the cart. Gillies guided Dobbin towards the grave. Prayers were said, so simple, yet meaningful. The earth was replaced, and a rough wooden cross was hammered into the ground. They all stood there in silence. The sun was warm and the sky now a clear blue. Gillies felt sad, yet happy that he had settled his father where he had been most happy. This was their area of the mountain range where his father had taught him the facts of life. This is where Bambi had been let free again. This was where he had found friendship with the fox.

This is where he had rested on his way to meet Charlotte. Yes, this was the right spot to let his father rest. When he and Charlotte were ready to have child, he would bring him to this camp, now a resting place, and commune with his father. He would, one day, tell his son about his grandfather. He had many tales to tell. On their trail back to the farmhouse, he told Charlotte what he had been thinking. She smiled as she squeezed his hand.

"What if we have a girl?" she mused.

"Then we will have more until we have a son." Was his quick response.

Mother joined them as they made their way back. She had made a wreath of wild flowers. It had been a sad, yet joyous, burial. She was happy that her man was resting in the mountains he loved. She knew that this was also the place where she could visit and talk with him. David had found comfort in the way it had been all so natural. Never in his wildest dream could he have believed he would have found a way of life that had such values in the meaning of life. They had all been naked as the day they were born. No rules to conform to and the words spoken were from the heart. Just a simple occasion, yet so beautiful and meaningful.

Gillies' regret was that his father had not lived to see how his own desire to live the simple life, was now to be shared by others. There was much work to be done now. Letters appeared in their mailbox weekly. Soon there would be no need to run the vegetable stall in the market. They would need all they could grow for naturist campers. Charlotte and Marian started to plan a little store for campers to shop from. Vegetables and fruit were in abundance. Gillies once a week would head off into the wilds to set traps to catch rabbits. Often Joseph would join him. Gillies enjoyed teaching him how to stalk wild boar and deer. The lessons his father had taught him echoed in his head. David was busy with trips to the market place selling vegetables. From there, he spread the word of their venture by word of mouth and leaflets he had had printed by the local newspaper press. Each time he returned to farmhouse, he would check the mailbox. His friends that he had met in Germany had received his letters at long last. He had asked them to spread the news about Gillies' venture. Now he was holding three letters in his hand, all were excitedly read over the meal that evening. Two letters were from interested naturists from German, and one from a family in Holland. So news was now spreading around. At weekends, the youths worked like beavers clearing natural areas for tents to be pitched. It was a joy watching them enjoying their freedom. Most evenings would find them sitting around their camp fire, naked and happy, playing cards and chatting.

Gillies missed his father. Often he would wander off to where he rested. He would sit and talk over life's problems, asking for advice. He had seen his father as being the one that had all answers to all things. Little Charlotte was becoming moody. Gillies could not work out if it was because she was missing her father too, or if she was missing some of her friends she had made at school. Had he done the right thing in   taking her away from all that? As for his mother, she seemed to go inward with her grief. Gillies were concerned about her. He had to be strong for both of them.

The first summer of opening mainly saw locals camping at weekends. The youths had done a good job of making clearings. Each clearing had ridge tent pitched. It was heart-warming for Gillies to wander around seeing small family groups cooking food over log fires, safely lit near their tents. A communal BBQ had been built. Most evenings, naturists would gather round cooking meat that had been bought from their little farm shop. It was good seeing how the village and town folk were brought together, enjoying their freedom. Entertainment was simple. Sometimes someone would surprise a small audience by playing a flute. Songs were sung, and jokes were told. The shop was making money now. Many an evening, Gillies and friends would sit around discussing investment into buying tents to make it attractive for those that could not provide their own. Soon the camp began to take shape. Ten tents were pitched in an area near the pool. When the first of the overseas visitors arrived, these tents were their homes for holiday periods. The sound of laughter could be heard coming from the pool, as families bathed and cooled themselves down from heat of the sun. It was going to be a good summer. In the evenings, Gillies and Charlotte often wandered around the tented areas. They loved the way couples and families, often with young children, sat around the camp fire just talking with others that had joined them.

It was now mid-way through the season when the first camp BBQ was lit. Naturists gathered around to watch the sardines placed on a mesh wire frame, then placed on the glowing embers. Smoke bellowed out and drifted away up into the sky. Tables were laid out with freshly made bread and bowls of salad. The sardines were dished out as the hungry campers offered their plates, and found a table to sit down at. There was a buzz of happy conversation and laugher as the feast was consumed. The sound of guitar music gently playing in the background added to the relaxed scene. To the true knowledgeable observer, this was a natural scene of naked free-spirited folk enjoying life shared with others. To many, this scene would seem strange. Gillies sat with his friends who had helped him to reach his dream. How he wished his father could be with him to enjoy the feeling of success that ran through his body now. As the evening went on, Gillies drifted away alone from the festivities. Charlotte sat there watching him. For a moment she felt that she should join him, but she knew he would want to be alone to visit his father's grave in the mountains. He had walked for over a mile before the singing and sound of the guitar playing was just faint to his ears. He sat there for a moment at the side of the grave.

There were tears in his eyes, and a guilty feeling in his heart. Why should his father not have been there to share the early days of the opening? Why should he be allowed to be so happy? He knew that this day was a day to be happy. Tomorrow was another day, as he was about to do battle with the local authorities over taking Little Charlotte away from school. He looked to the heavens for help and guidance from his father. The father that had truly believed in nature's ways of giving true values to one's life. A heavy black cloud had been drifting across the moon's face. Now suddenly the area around the grave seemed to brighten. He spent quite some time with his father. Each time he asked a question, there seemed to be something around him that provided an answer. First the brightness of the moon, then a breeze of wind rustled the leaves from the trees, and the sound of a night owl. It was strange how people, including himself, missed out on these signs that nature offered up in times of doubt. As he prepared to leave his father's grave, his friendly fox pushed his head out through the bushes. They both stared at each other for a while. It was as if even the fox was confirming the thoughts he was leaving with. The journey home seemed to be shorter in time. He knew now that his father had most of the answers. All he had to do was to build on the strengths his father had given him. He was greeted by Charlotte as he wandered through the barn doors. She could tell he and his father had been as one again. That night they made love like they had never made love before. Now, for the first time, they were sure they wanted to make child. The thrusts that Gillies gave out on the final climax were so forceful that they both knew that this was the night of all nights. They lay there naked and exhausted form their love making. They talked about the future and the problems that lay ahead. Somehow though, they were a lot more sure of themselves. Sleep overtook them. Their doubts faded with sleep. Tomorrow they would deal with the problems that lay ahead.

SEVENTEEN

It was another hot sunny day. Gillies was helping David build the last stage of a toilet block. They had mused about the blessings of it being for naturists. The showers were communal, which made it much easier to build. Even the toilets were the same for both. They laughed at the way the trough like men's urinals were exposed to the elements with only a shelter type roof. This was a way of life that educated the minds of the young way ahead of town's people. They were both standing back admiring their work when they heard the rumble of cartwheels in the distance. Gillies squinted his eyes against the glare of the sun. He recognized the cart with its official riders aboard. The local councillors were making a visit. Gillies looked at David. They both took a deep breath as they made their way back to the farmhouse where the cart of officials were about to dismount. That stare at their naked bodies said it all.

"So, you are still leading your native ways then."

Gillies smiled at the stupidity of the remark. He stood proud and motionless, just staring at the official.

The official snorted as he felt inside his jacket pocket trying to pull out a document. He looked yet again at Gillies. He glanced around the now assembled friends of Gillies. His fellow officials began to climb down from the cart to join him.

"Where is your father?" The official asked.

Gillies choose his words well. He knew this question was going to be asked.

"He is here."

"Where?"

"He is up in the mountains." Gillies replied, looking over his shoulder.

"We can wait for him to return." The official said, tapping the papers on his thigh.

"You haven't got that amount of time." David said, smiling at his own quick response.

The officials were now beginning to feel uncomfortable, surrounded by eight naked people to their four. The leading official suddenly thrust the papers into Gillies hand.

"Give that to your father. He has to be made aware that this is a legal document demanding that his daughter has to attend school.

Failure to do, then he could find himself being in contempt of court. He could find himself being fined and maybe sent to prison."

Gillies could not refrain from laughing. This became infectious, and all his friends joined in laughing at the ludicrous situation.

"The best I can do is to read this document to my father."

The official looked puzzled at Gillies statement, yet chose not to question him. The official party climbed up onto the cart again, the reins were slapped across the horse's hind quarters, and the cart headed away from the farmhouse at a pace. Gillies smiled at the end result. He would take the papers to his father's grave and honour his words of reading the document to his father. What would happen after that was impossible to contemplate. At least it gave him time to think through this problem. As for Little Charlotte, she was unaware of all that was taking place. His mother was worried, although Gillies had tried to keep the worries away from her as her own health was failing fast. Gillies knew that she was still in shock over losing her husband. If only the outside world would allow them to lead their own lives. David spent many hours trying to console Gillies. The best answer was to let his mother and sister return to town life again. Gillies was unsure that this was the best way to solve the problem. He talked to Charlotte. She knew that her parents would be willing to take them back into their home again. It was turning out to be the best solution in the end. A week passed, and many times Gillies and his mother had gone over and over the situation. With heavy hearts, Gillies and Charlotte had set off to meet her parents. It was a blessing in disguise at the timing of this. As they were sitting there with her parents in their sitting room, Charlotte, having heard her parents agreeing to help again, she suddenly announced that she was with child. This was something that she had held back from Gillies ears. Suddenly there were tears of joy and hugs all around at the news. Gillies was overjoyed and immediately concerned about how she was feeling. Her mother assured him that all was well. Her daughter was strong and healthy. Gillies sat there feeling so clever about his part in the proceedings. Now he was really a man. On the return journey home, he steered Dobbin around nearly all uneven parts of the road. At the slightest bump, he would worriedly ask if Charlotte was feeling well. She would only smile at his concern. Several reassuring kisses calmed his fears. Within the week,

Gillies' mother and Little Charlotte where settled in the town again. Gillies would have liked to have challenged the authorities over the morals of having Little Charlotte educated by his mother, in the same way she had him. How he hated the officials and their lack of understanding. How he wished that somehow it was possible to get these small-minded people to take time off out of their lives to at least experience his way of life. Now that he had conformed to their wishes, Little Charlotte settled down to school work. Many tears had been wiped dry as she tried to understand why she could not stay at the farmhouse. Gillies was worried about his mother's health. He had seen how worry had affected her health. Now though, he had many things to deal with. The camp site had to be developed. The interest in the lifestyle was growing. The post-box seemed to have to be emptied more often now. Requests for details kept David busy.

Mike Herring

Footnote

Mike had the pleasure of meeting the main character in the book when he was producing a documentary film on the naturist lifestyle. His story of how this man, *at the time in his fifties*, had lived his life with nature, Mike felt it just had to be told. Whilst the story is mainly true, the author allowed his creative mind to add to the storyline.

ALSO AVAILABLE WITH GREEN CAT BOOKS

LISA J RIVERS
Winding Down

Follow Samantha's path of self-destruction, dogged by good luck, in Lisa's first novel, a black comedy

Why I Have So Many Cats

Lisa's first book is a bitter-sweet poetry book about the many cats that have owned her over the years.

ALSO AVAILABLE WITH GREEN CAT BOOKS

LUNA FELIS
Life Well Lived

There are two things that are guaranteed - birth and death. Few of us are ready for the latter, but sometimes putting things into order can put our minds at rest. Things we wish we had said to someone, but never had the time or courage.

Luna has designed this book like a scrapbook, for the owner to complete in their own time, focusing on what they would like in the event of their passing. Last wishes, memories and important information are sections included within the book.

ALSO AVAILABLE WITH GREEN CAT BOOKS

GABRIEL EZIOROBO
Words Of My Mouth

Gabriel is a Nigerian poet and contemporary freelance writer. Words of My Mouth is a poetry book about the world around us, the things we see on or countries.

The Brain Behind Freelance Writing

Gabriel has composed a pocket size guide with hints and tips about how to be a freelance writer.

ARE YOU A WRITER?

We are looking for writers to send in their manuscripts.

If you would like to submit your work, please send to

books@green-cat.co

www.green-cat.co/books

Printed in Great Britain
by Amazon